To Olive, Eliza, and Roxy
May they know no fear

Published by Sourcebooks Jabberwocky, an imprint of Sourcebooks, Inc.
P.O. Box 4410, Naperville, Illinois 60567-4410
(630) 961-3900
Fax: (630) 961-2168
www.jabberwockykids.com

Originally published in 2014 in the United Kingdom by Oxford University Press, an imprint of Oxford University Press.

Library of Congress Cataloging-in-Publication data is on file with the publisher.

Source of Production: Worzalla, Stevens Point WI, USA
Date of Production: August 2014
Run Number: 50002032

Printed and bound in the United States of America.
WOZ 10 9 8 7 6 5 4 3 2 1

YOUNG HOUDINI

The Magician's Fire

SIMON NICHOLSON

sourcebooks
jabberwocky

Author's Note

Harry Houdini was a magician and escape artist like no other. At the dawn of the twentieth century, he traveled the globe, subjecting himself to spectacular and terrifying ordeals, the likes of which had simply never been seen before.

He escaped from nailed-shut crates thrown to the bottom of icy lakes. He writhed his way out of a straitjacket while dangling from a bridge more than 200 feet high. Lashed to the front of a loaded cannon, he sprung from the ropes just before the fuse detonated the charge; incarcerated by Europe's most ruthless police force in their cruelest prison, he mocked them by walking miraculously free. Nothing defeated him—and no one could explain his mysterious powers.

Who was Harry Houdini and how did he acquire such phenomenal skills? I couldn't stop thinking about what might have happened to him as a boy to turn him into such an extraordinary man.

All great stories have a great beginning. This is the story of Houdini: the boy magician.

MANHATTAN, 1886

Chapter 1

THE TRAIN WAS COMING. Harry could see the puffs of blackened steam rising over a row of broken-down houses. He could hear the clatter of the engine. Down by his feet, vibrations were wobbling along the iron rails, and the ragged hems of his trousers were wobbling too. *Won't be long now.* He stood there a little longer, his boot-polish-stained fingers twitching, his eyes narrowing in the direction of the thundering roar.

He tugged a sturdy-looking padlock out of his jacket pocket and continued chaining himself to the spot in the middle of the track.

"You've really lost it this time, Harry!"

"Harry! Are you absolutely sure about this?"

A boy and a girl stood just a few paces away. Billie, the girl, wore a ragged, glue-spattered factory smock and was leaning casually against a concrete stump, her head cocked to one side, an eyebrow raised. *Typical, not even the tiniest bit impressed,* thought Harry with a smile, glancing across at the boy, who was a far more satisfying sight. Arthur was completely beside himself with excitement, hopping from foot to foot, his neatly tailored tweed suit flapping, his hands racing through a copy of the *New York City Train Timetable.*

"Do you really think this is a good idea, Harry? My calculations have turned out right, you see." Stitches popped in the tweed suit and the younger boy's tie swirled as he flung an arm toward the puffs of smoke. "That's the 3:24 from Grand Central. Which by my estimate is due to hit this exact spot…" He tugged a pocket watch from his waistcoat, dangled it in front of his face, and stared at it with eyes the size of half-dollar coins. "…in exactly two minutes and twenty-seven seconds!"

"So we have to hurry, Artie!" Harry looped a chain around his left leg, pulled it up around his head, and adjusted it so that it was at a jaunty angle. He heard his voice echo around, still full of the accent of his faraway Hungarian home, so different from his friend's English tones. "Good job on the calculations, but I'm not even properly manacled yet! Another chain, Billie?"

"One of the really heavy ones? Or perhaps something a little lighter, sir?" Another grin and Billie pushed off the concrete stump, reached into the sack at her feet, and yanked out a clinking length of iron. "I managed to find you a nice selection, heavy ones, light ones, that sort of thing…" Her voice bounced along with drawls and twangs as she swung the chain around a bit. "Any other deadly situations you'd like me and Artie to rustle up for you? Dangle you by a rope off the Brooklyn Bridge? Or smuggle you into the lion's cage at the Central Park menagerie, maybe? We're getting pretty good now. I'm sure we could do it…"

"You'd do a great job, both of you, but can we talk about it later?" Harry wrapped the chain around his middle, making sure that it also was at a jaunty angle. "Let's just concentrate on the Great Train—"

"The Great Train Escape, I know." Billie's left eyebrow lifted a little higher. "Hey, Artie, seeing as we're busy with trains today, did I ever tell you about my own brush with one? The Louisiana Express Hay Wagon Ride, that's what I call it, and it was pretty rough…"

"There's no time, Billie!" Harry slid the padlock through the links.

"Sure there's time! So, I was desperate for a ride, and so I hung out on a bridge near a freight station, waiting. When the train rattled underneath with a load of wagons of hay, I just jumped down! Nearly broke a leg!" Billie reached behind her back, pulled around the little ukulele she kept strapped there, and started strumming a tune. "But that's what it's like on the road. You've got to grab any chance you can. So there I was, riding all the way to Arkansas, strumming my uke, and—"

"Billie! Not now! Everyone's waiting. Look!"

Harry snapped the padlock shut and managed to jerk his head toward the crowd of about fifteen people lined up along the top of the bank on the far side of the tracks, framed against the blue September sky. Passersby, shopkeepers, and even a couple of washerwomen—Billie and Arthur had spent nearly an hour drumming them up by racing around the surrounding streets. Every one of them seemed gripped by what was going on, their gazes fixed in his direction. *They'll stare even harder now*, Harry thought as he plucked the key from the padlock and sent it flying through the air. It vanished into a patch of thorny bushes some distance away.

"You've really done it." Billie's ukulele playing stopped. Even she was looking impressed now, staring after the key.

"Exactly!" Harry jerked his head toward the crowd. "That's what everyone's thinking!"

"Yes, but you really *have* done it!" Arthur was a high-speed hopping, page-flicking, watch-waggling blur. "We'll never be able to find it in all those thorns!"

"It's all part of the act." Harry breathed deeply and stared at the padlock as hard as he could. "Look, I shouldn't really be talking—I'm supposed to be pretending to have magical powers."

He kept doing just that. The clattering roar was louder now. The rails were vibrating faster, and his ragged trouser hems were flapping faster, but he didn't bother about any of those things. Instead, he kept staring at the chains with that deliberately mysterious gaze. He even tugged the padlock up to his mouth and muttered to it.

See a boy free himself through the speaking of ancient charms. That was what Billie and Arthur had told the crowd—and from the excited gasps he could hear drifting from the bank, it sounded like his audience was well on the way to believing it too.

Harry kept muttering to the padlock, deliberately using phrases of Hungarian, knowing that the unfamiliar words would sound particularly mysterious to the listening crowd. He muttered even louder and made his eyes roll about, pretending to lose himself completely in a magical trance, even as he detected faint odors of oil and soot curling up his nose—

"The train! The train!"

Harry's eyes stopped rolling. They flicked toward the crowd. Every one of those fifteen heads had swiveled to the left because the train had shot out from behind the buildings and was curving steadily around the track. Arms pointed, faces turned white. The engine, a hurtling bulk of iron, was still several hundred yards away, but steam shrieked from it as it clanged along the rails, and it was gathering speed. Harry watched it. The odors of oil and soot weren't just curling up his nose now. They were snaking down into his mouth, flavoring the spit trickling down his throat. *Time to get a move on.* But he couldn't resist squeezing in just a bit more bug-eyed magical staring at the chains.

"Harry! You've left it too late!"

A yell from Arthur as he raced for the thorny bushes. Billie was pulling off a well-rehearsed swoon, tottering about with the back of a hand against her forehead. *Nicely done*, thought Harry, as he watched Billie collapse onto the gravel. Meanwhile Artie arrived at the bush and started rooting about as if all was lost. *All part of the act.*

Still, they had been right earlier—there wasn't any way they could find the key and run back to set him free before the train hit. The thought made the chains holding him in place feel particularly heavy. Under his threadbare shirt, he felt a drop of sweat glide down between his shoulder blades. *Yes, time to get a move on...*

"Stop the train!"

"Somebody *do* something!"

Screams from the crowd. One of the washerwomen had dropped her basket, the clothes inside tumbling down the bank, but no one seemed to have noticed. *Utterly gripped.* More drops of sweat were gathering now on his forehead, his neck, under his arms, and Harry could feel strange little twitches quivering through his body. *Good*—every twitch, every drop of sweat would help him concentrate on the trick that lay ahead.

He lifted the padlock to his mouth again and muttered a bit more of that spell. He surrounded the padlock with his hands so no one would see the tiny bulge in his upper lip as his tongue curled up inside. Harry closed his eyes and felt his tongue deftly fetch down the little bent nail that was lodged there and nudge it around until it was gripped between his teeth. The bent end poked out of the corner of his mouth and he shot it into the padlock's keyhole.

Concentrate.

Harry tilted his head. He had carefully bent the nail so it fit the padlock perfectly. He had practiced endless times, first with his hands, then with his mouth. But he still felt his jaw shudder slightly as it shifted so that the nail angled upward. His brain throbbed with the clatter of iron wheels, the shriek of steam. *Concentrate, concentrate.* He stared straight at the train, just a hundred yards away now, as he continued picking the lock. And then the nail slipped.

Unexpectedly, the padlock had jerked to the left, tugging the nail from his teeth. For a couple of seconds, the little length of metal balanced precariously on his lower lip. He felt his whole body turn cold as he tried to fetch it back with his tongue. His vision blurred and he realized that his eyes had crossed, struggling to hold the nail in view as it balanced such a short distance away. His tongue strained, and the twitches raced through every part of him.

Concentrate.

The nail was back between his teeth. He shot it back into the lock again, his jaw re-angling. He checked the train, which had jammed on its brakes but was hurtling forward anyway, an iron blur, just forty yards away. *Thirty, twenty.* The brakes screeched, but all he could hear from deep inside the padlock was the stretching of tiny springs, the grind of tiny levers.

Then, echoing out of the keyhole, a click.

The clasp sprang open. The chains, heavy and cold, slithered away from him. One of them snagged on his left elbow but he shook it off, shaking off the other chains too, sending them flying away from the track. He looked up and saw the train's vast front racing toward him. His legs, he had to admit, were a little less steady than usual, but he managed to spring into the air, just in time, and thudded onto the gravel next to the tracks.

He tucked the nail back inside his lip. Briefly, he remembered that troubling moment when it had dangled so precariously, and took in a shaky breath. But then he jumped up, brushing the dust from his clothes. He stumbled away from the track, his ragged clothes billowing in the thundering breeze of the train's cars as they clattered past, picking up speed again.

Ahead of him was the crowd. Everyone was clapping, cheering, waving hats in the air, and throwing coins in his direction. Harry stopped walking and stood there for some time, watching the coins land.

The train was gone now, but he still stood there. His vision blurred, and for a while he stopped thinking of anything other than his still-pounding heart, his still-trembling body. Then he felt something jab him in his side.

"Harry? We are *here*, you know?"

It was Billie. She was standing next to him, laughing, and her elbow was doing the jabbing, quite hard. Harry blinked and then looked around at Arthur, who was on his other side, a smile on his face too.

"Sorry." Harry blinked again and felt his face grow warm. "Sometimes takes me a bit of time to come around—"

"Don't worry. We're used to it." Billie rolled her eyes.

"Thanks." Harry held out his hands. "So anyway—let's give them what they want, shall we?"

He waited for his friends to grab his hands. Then, together with them, he performed the move that he had practiced more than any other.

A slow, elegant bow.

Chapter 2

HARRY RAN ACROSS THE park. Light was just starting to fade from the sky, and the last wisps of soot and engine oil had cleared from his clothes. His boots thudded over the cool grass and a wooden shoeshine box swung from his shoulder, rattling with the cans and brushes inside. Flipping open the box's lid, he checked one of its compartments and snapped the lid shut again. Leaping over a railing, he took a shortcut through a flower bed, ran across another stretch of grass, and joined Billie, hiding behind a rhododendron bush.

"Is it ready, Harry?"

"Sure is!"

"Exactly the way we ordered it? Every last detail?"

"Every last one! Good thing the train trick went down so well just now. We'd never have had enough otherwise." He tugged out the lining of his trouser pocket, empty of coins. "That's got to be the craziest trick yet, huh?"

"You bet, Harry. No doubt about it." Billie peered back through the bush. "He's still in there, by the way. Hasn't come out since we said good-bye."

Harry joined her in peering through the twigs and leaves. A short distance away, a brilliantly white building towered beside the park, its windows shining, marble steps running up to its front door. Harry checked the windows, inspecting them for any sign of movement inside. But, as usual, the whole house was eerily still.

"So how did you find out, Billie?" Harry turned back. "That it's his birthday, I mean."

"Mentioned it to me a couple of months ago. 'The seventeenth of September,' he said, and that's today."

"But how come he didn't say anything earlier? The train trick was all he wanted to talk about!"

"He loves our tricks, doesn't he? Probably grateful we were doing one—must have helped take his mind off it. Still, his mind'll be back on it now. Wait, there he is!"

Harry peered again. Billie was right—the front door was opening, and Arthur was stepping out. And she was right about something else too. Arthur's mind was clearly no longer on anything to do with their tricks. The younger boy's movements were slow and his head was lowered as he trod down the steps, wandered down the sidewalk, and crossed the street into the park. Harry even heard a faint sigh drifting through the air. He glanced at Billie, who nodded, and just as Arthur reached the bush, they strolled out.

"Hi, Artie!"

"Billie? Harry?" Artie stopped and blinked at them. "I thought you were both working this evening!"

"Turns out I'm not due at the factory just yet." Billie adjusted her cap, which was every bit as glue-spattered as her smock. "And you're not planning to shine any shoes for the next couple of hours or so either, are you, Harry?"

"Thought I'd leave it awhile," said Harry, shrugging.

"Oh." Arthur looked puzzled. "Well, I'm not doing anything very exciting, I'm afraid. Just going for a quick walk around the park. Before"—he stared back at the house—"going back inside again."

"We'll go for a walk with you, Artie." Billie tugged his arm. "Come on."

They set off across the park. Billie reached for her ukulele, strung across her back as usual, but seemed to change her mind, and Harry knew why. She, like him, had seen the first signs of that familiar kink forming

13

on their friend's forehead. At the same time, Arthur's left hand was reaching down to his jacket pocket, drawing out a little ribbon of paper with letters and dots running along it. Harry kept walking and tried to think of what to say.

"Heading off to Chicago, is he?" Billie got there first. "Like you expected?"

"First thing tomorrow." Arthur ran a finger along the dots. "He sent this message through from his office yesterday, telling the servants. The machine in the hallway hammered it out, along with the usual stuff about stocks and shares. Servants read it and left it in the wastepaper basket, as usual."

"I just don't get it." Billie put her hand on Arthur's shoulder. "He just got back from a trip to… Where was it again?"

"Washington," said Arthur. "He was gone three weeks."

"I mean, it's one thing to spend all your time in an office in the city where you actually live—but traveling all over the country?" Billie shook her head.

"He's got meetings, hasn't he? That's what it's like if you come to America to set up a brand-new bank." Arthur frowned. "It's been this way ever since we moved to New York, and that's eight months now.

Mind you, he totally ignored me in London too. As long as I can remember, he's been just the same. Work comes first, a nice expensive house comes second, and having a bunch of servants who do exactly what he wants is important too." He swung back toward the house. "Me, I'm just expected to tag along."

His eyes narrowed. Harry swung around too and saw why. As daylight faded, lamps were being lit inside the grand front room of the brilliantly white building. Inside stood Lord Trilby-Roberts, Arthur's father. Tall, stiff, and wearing an immaculately tailored suit, the rich banker was standing perfectly straight and talking on a new invention called a telephone, while staring out through the window with an expression that, even at this distance, seemed cold and aloof. Around him, various servants busily gathered papers and files, no doubt in preparation for the trip to Chicago.

"So he's just going to…leave you again?" Harry turned back. "To hang around in that house?"

"Along with all his other stuff." Artie kept staring at the window. "Antique furniture, clocks from Switzerland, that sort of thing."

"Good thing he installed the ticker-tape machine," Billie said. "Least that way you get warning of what he's planning."

"I know," said Arthur. "I know."

He reached back into his pocket and drew out another ribbon, gripping its end with particular force.

"Actually, the machine hammered out another message this morning." His hand tightened until the knuckles were white. "Something I wasn't expecting—today of all days."

"Really?" Peering at the ribbon, Billie looked hopeful.

"Found it crumpled up in the trash, just like the others. Do the servants really think I won't find them?"

"It was from your father in his office? To the servants back home?"

"Of course."

"And it arrived today? The seventeenth of September?"

"Yes."

"And it's about you?"

"Certainly is."

"So what is it? What does it say?"

"It's instructions to the servants about contacting another boarding school," said Arthur, and he crumpled the ribbon into a tiny, hard ball. His eyes were curiously bright as his thumb and finger gripped the tiny paper ball. Harry wasn't sure what to say at all, and neither, from the look of her, was Billie.

16

"Boarding school?" She managed something, at last. "Sounds grim. Still, at least that's taking some kind of interest in you…"

"Not really. There are different sorts of boarding schools, for a start. The one Father has in mind is the sort of place you send someone if you specifically intend to take no interest in them whatsoever for as long as you possibly can. Hard for me to be even the tiniest distraction to him if I've been sent miles away." Arthur held up the ball of paper and glared at it. "The school's in Dayton, Ohio. So that's 452 miles away, to be precise."

"So what are you going to do?" Billie looked genuinely worried. "We don't want you disappearing anywhere, Artie."

"Me neither. What, and not see the two people who *do* actually take an interest in me? I don't think so." Artie flicked the ball furiously away. "I'll use the normal tricks. I've foiled all the other attempts to send me away and I'll foil this one too, don't you worry. It's just it's a bit much, him doing this. On my… On my b…"

He stopped. He sat down on a bench, hard. The paper ball was bouncing down the path, and he stared after it, his hands shoved in his tweed trouser pockets.

As bad as we've ever seen him, thought Harry, and he turned back to the white house again. The tall, rigid figure was still there, the telephone in his hand, his servants bustling obediently around him. Harry's eyes narrowed, just as his friend's had done. Then he turned back to Billie who, with a determined look on her face, had plunked herself down on the bench, right next to Arthur.

"Don't worry, Artie." She thumped him on the shoulder. "We've got you a birthday treat. Pass the blindfold, Harry!"

"Birthday—how d'you know it was my birthday? *Oof!*"

The blindfold was from Harry's shoeshine box. A perfectly clean rag, he had bought it specially, and he swiftly pulled it over Arthur's eyes and knotted it around the back of his head. Arthur's hands flailed as Billie hoisted him over her shoulder and staggered off across the park.

"Where are you taking me? What's going on—*Hey!* That tickles!"

"You've always said you wanted to be a magician's assistant!" Harry ran on ahead. "Wearing the occasional blindfold's part of it. Ready to row, Billie?"

He jumped into the little boat moored at the edge

of the pond. Billie tottered up to it and Harry helped her in, catching Arthur and propping him on one of the seats. Billie leaped in and grabbed an oar, and Harry grabbed one too. Together, they started to row, picking up speed quickly and passing various ducks.

"What is going on?" Arthur, still blindfolded, was laughing now.

"You're in the hands of an expert, birthday boy." Billie sculled to the left. "Not as if I haven't blindfolded someone before. Tied her up too! The owner of my orphanage, down in New Orleans."

"You've told us this, Billie!" Harry rowed faster.

"Now that was a real rough business, and I'd only just gotten started then—the Knotted Sheet Dangle, that's what I call it—not only did I have to deal with the scariest owner of an orphanage there ever was, next I had to jump out the window and climb down a rope of knotted sheets, all the way down to the street below and—*Watch out!*"

The boat thudded into the side of the dock. Harry threw the mooring rope, lassoed the mooring post, and helped Billie pull Arthur out. It was Harry's turn to hoist the younger boy onto his shoulder now, and he stumbled out through the park gate and climbed onto a horse-drawn omnibus. He and

19

Billie sat down, and for the next twenty minutes, they clattered across Manhattan, watching the city shudder past the window and laughing at the odd looks the other passengers were giving them, two scruffy street kids with a blindfolded boy in a tweed suit squashed between them. The omnibus tilted to a halt, and together they hoisted their friend and carried him out onto the street. On the other side, they saw their destination.

A small, rather grimy-looking diner.

They burst in through the door, the bell somersaulting above them. They carried Arthur to a table, propped him on a chair, and drew up chairs of their own. Harry nodded to a waitress, who rattled a little wooden cart over to them. She picked up what was on it and lowered it onto the table. At the same moment, Harry and Billie removed Arthur's blindfold.

"Happy birthday, Artie!"

A cake. Chocolate icing spiraled on its sides. Cream oozed from its center, spilling onto the plate, and three layers of sponge cake could be detected, each one sitting on a thick layer of yet more icing. Blinking as his eyes adjusted to the light, Artie took in all these details, but one seemed to affect him in particular: written on the cake's top in sugary sprinkles was his name, along with a skillfully frosted picture of a stack of interesting-looking books.

"But how did you afford this?" Arthur gasped.

"The money from the trick, silly," Billie replied.

"But…that's Harry's money, really. He stood in front of th—"

"That's not how we do things, Artie. You know that," Harry interrupted. "You calculated the train time, didn't you? Billie found the chains, and both of you ran around drumming up that crowd…"

"With no crowd, there wouldn't *be* any money," agreed Billie, grabbing a spoon.

"Exactly. So we split the money three ways." Harry leaned forward and jabbed a finger on the tablecloth. "Anyway, who knows where I'd have gotten with my tricks if it hadn't been for you encouraging me, Artie. Remember when you saw me trying to cross Sixth Avenue by leaping between speeding streetcars? I was going nowhere then. Just some shoeshine boy, leaping about—no one else was noticing. But then you wandered up and told me all about that book you'd been reading in the library…"

"*Fire Dances in the Amazon*," said Arthur quietly.

"Magicians there prove their skills by dancing through pits of fire! Why not do the same, flying through the showers of sparks from the streetcars?" Harry turned to Billie, his finger still firm on the tablecloth. "Same goes for you, Billie. You saw me practicing tightrope-walking along the back of that park bench—"

"Waved my arms around, trying to make you lose balance." Billie smiled.

"Like I say, at least you noticed. And you also had the idea of stringing a rope way up high between two trees and getting me to walk along it while muttering spells and wriggling my arms free of no less than twenty-five knots. Helped me practice it over and over too, and *that* was how we drew our first crowd." The finger was hurting now from all the jabbing. "So anyway, that's why we split stuff in three. And because it's your birthday, Artie, me and Billie decided to spend our shares on something you'd like."

"So that just left your bit. And we decided to throw that in too, if that's all right by you," Billie added.

"Yes, of course..." Arthur's voice had gone very quiet indeed. "Thanks, folks..."

For some time, he said nothing more. He just sat there, staring at the cake. Uncertain what to do next, Harry didn't move either. The silence went on for so long that the icing melting under the top layer of the cake began to tilt it to one side. Harry and Billie exchanged worried looks. Then, finally, Arthur reached out a hand and picked up the knife.

"Father can ignore me as much as he likes and send as many messages as he wants about boarding schools too." He smiled. "The three of us—we've got some serious eating to do."

The cake flew apart. Arthur cut the first slice, and then cut two more for Billie and Harry, and then kept cutting more slices for all three of them, in between gobbling down what was on his plate. Spoons flashed, hands grabbed, bits of sponge cake bounced across the table, and Harry saw one of the customers at a nearby table duck as a blob of icing hurtled right by him.

Finally, no more slices were left, just a few crumbs and smears of icing, and these were busily devoured as well, Billie even holding her plate up to her face and rotating it so that her tongue could lick up every last trace. At last, they were done, and they tilted back their chairs and wiped a few last smears from their mouths.

"Deee-licious!" said Billie.

"The best cake I've ever tasted." Arthur nodded. "And it's the best birthday I can remember as well."

"And that, Artie," said Harry, leaning back in his

chair farthest of all, "was well worth standing in front of a hurtling train for!"

He meant every word. He had meant the words earlier too. And he wasn't the only one who felt that way, it seemed, because just then he felt his hand grow warm and realized that Arthur had taken hold of it. The tweed-suited boy also took hold of Billie's hand, and then Billie reached across and grabbed the only hand that remained on the table, Harry's other one. The three of them sat there, the business of the diner clattering around them. No trace of sadness on Artie's face now. It was smiling all over, and Billie was smiling as well, and Harry felt his own face break into a grin.

His eyes flicked up to the diner's clock. Then to the grimy window. Through it, a familiar spindly shape could be seen, hovering by a lamppost.

"Your birthday treat's not over yet, Artie!" Harry scraped back his chair. "It's only just beginning!"

"Really?" Arthur looked around, confused.

"I think *I* know what Harry's talking about." Turning, Billie could clearly see the spindly shape too. "I see him," she said.

"See him? See who?" Arthur swiveled around in his seat, trying to see.

"Herbie," said Harry. "He came!"

Chapter ③

HARRY, ARTHUR, AND BILLIE raced across the street toward the elderly figure by the lamp post.

"Hello, Herbie!"

The old man turned around. His gray hair drooped, his movements were slow, and his clothes billowed around his limbs as he gripped his walking cane. Harry leaped onto the curb, balanced there, and waited for the complicated wrinkles of Herbie's face to arrange themselves into a smile.

"Harry." There it was. "Half past six, just as we agreed."

"Did you bring the tickets? It's Artie's birthday, remember!"

"Of course." The smile hung there as three rectangular stubs of paper flowered in Herbie's hand. He handed them over and started walking slowly down the street, his cane tapping. "Three tickets for tonight's performance. I assume you wish to watch me for the usual reason?"

"You bet, Mr. Lemster!" Billie hurried up, Arthur just behind. "Why else would Harry want to see a magician?"

"Maybe we could go into the theater with you? Seeing as it's my birthday?" Arthur walked along, trying to sound innocent. "Just to have a look backstage..."

"Ah, that would be quite against the rules, Arthur." The old man gripped his cane. "I never let anyone behind the curtain. You know that. You won't attempt to meet me at the stage door after the show either, I trust?" He stopped. "That is our agreement. What if your keen eyes spotted some trace of a trick, a clue, that might remain upon me... That would be most unfair..."

"Harry'd be looking, that's for sure." Arthur nodded. "He's seen a whole bunch of other magicians since we last met, Herbie—Chinese conjurers, Russian tricksters, Indian illusionists, you name them. Discovered something from pretty much every one of them too."

"*Stole*, you mean," said Billie, laughing.

"Oh, it's not stealing, young Billie." Another smile from Herbie. "It's the whole business of trickery. A game that's been going on nearly a thousand years,

I'd say. We magicians, we're all studying each other, watching each other, keenly hunting for the slightest clue, the slightest trace of each other's devices. The flick of a thumb? The dart of an arm? An ingeniously placed trapdoor? Whatever it is, if we find it fair and square, it's ours to use." A scratching sound from his pocket and his hand rose, a flaming match gripped between finger and thumb. "A game. And young Harry's got the knack for it."

"Sure do." Harry watched as the flame quadrupled in size and then flew into the magician's mouth. He also saw the tiny flutter of a finger, which snuffed out the flame just as the lips closed. "I spotted that trick first time I met you, Herbie."

"Ah, but perhaps I saw you looking?" The old magician winked as he drew the match, flaming even more brightly, out of his ear. "Perhaps I spotted you in the crowd, with your ragged clothes and shoeshine box. Perhaps I observed, from the shape of your face and the accent in your voice, that you might come from the east of Europe too, a region most famous for its tricksters and illusionists." Another wink. "Perhaps I decided to angle myself so that you saw the device. To introduce you to the world of magic and all that it can be…"

"Doesn't explain how I picked it up so quickly." Down by his side, Harry's fingers were twitching, mimicking the device, that deft finger flutter, and his body flinched too, as he remembered the time of that first meeting in the middle of last winter, just a few weeks after he had arrived in New York. A penniless shoeshine boy, that was all he had been then, without a friend in the whole city, struggling to earn a living on the freezing sidewalks.

"Stayed up late that night, practicing the trick, and woke up with a few scorch marks on my lips the next morning. Right away, I started doing it! Bit of a shock for the gents whose shoes I was shining, to look down and see... Herbie?"

He peered closely at the old man. He always seemed a bit frail, but this was something different. Herbie's collar was damp with sweat, even though the evening air was perfectly cool, and the tips of his fingers were trembling. Tiny signs, and neither Billie nor Arthur seemed to have noticed them. But Harry had, and he tried to look for more, only to find the old magician staring straight back at him. The trembling stopped, and Herbie Lemster's eyes started flicking over Harry instead.

"Miraculously escaped from an oncoming train, did we?" The old man walked on.

"How'd you know that?" Billie butted in.

"Faint bruising around Harry's wrists, Billie. Some tightly looped chains, I'll wager..." Herbie lifted a finger, almost steady now, and pointed. "Although the main clue is the distinct smell of engine oil drifting from young Harry's clothes, mingling with the usual boot polish. Given that, and knowing our young friend's tastes for excitement..." He managed a smile. "Spotting little clues, tiny traces—that's what we magicians are good at, you see."

"He only just got away with it, Mr. Lemster!" Arthur said. "The crowd went totally wild!"

"Ah yes, the threat of genuine danger..." Herbie nodded, his cane tapping ahead of him. "Mind you, danger can enter a magician's life in so many ways."

Something was definitely up. The old man's fingers were trembling again, and more perspiration gleamed on his skin. These signs seemed to become even more pronounced, Harry observed, the further Herbie shuffled along the street. Glancing across at Billie and Arthur, he saw that they had noticed Herbie's distress too, because they had fallen silent and were staring at the old man closely. Reaching the end of the street and turning the corner, Herbie covered the last few yards toward the rickety old building looming across the street.

The Wesley Jones Theater. Its walls were crumbling, its windows lopsided, and faded posters hung on its signboards advertising its regular acts, one of which was a certain Herbie Lemster, Magician. An excited crowd was already gathered outside, forming a line to buy tickets, as Harry watched his elderly friend heading off toward the theater's stage door.

"Mr. Lemster?" Billie called out after him. "Are you feeling all right?"

Herbie swung around to face them. No question that something was up now. His clothes shuddered, drops of sweat gathered in those complicated wrinkles, and Herbie's face had turned strangely pale. And yet, obvious though those signs were, the words the old magician said next did nothing to explain them or even acknowledge that they existed.

"Good luck... Good luck with the world of magic..." he stammered, eyes wide and shimmering. "And all that it can be."

And with that, the old man turned and disappeared into the Wesley Jones Theater.

Chapter 4

HARRY SAT DOWN IN the theater. The insides were dilapidated, the seats broken, the curtain grubby and moth-eaten, but the audience was bustling and excited, waiting to see their favorite acts. Harry dropped his shoeshine box by his feet and prepared to go to work which, given what had just happened, wasn't going to be easy.

"So what do you think is up with him?" Billie dropped into the next seat and kicked her boots up onto the back of the one in front. "He looked really odd."

"I hope he's all right." Arthur settled himself too. "Herbie got you started, Harry. If he hadn't done that, maybe none of us would have met."

"It's true." Billie turned to Harry. "You might never have practiced tightrope-walking on that park bench, and I'd never have picked you out."

"Same for me and the streetcar-jumping stuff." Arthur nodded.

"It could all be part of the act. Herbie could be doing it deliberately as a distraction." Harry had cobbled this explanation together on the way in, and he was trying to get used to it. "He thinks that I'll worry about how he's acting and miss any little clue that might give his tricks away. It's pretty clever of ol' Herbie if you think about it."

His friends looked at him. Billie's eyebrows were raised rather high and Arthur was frowning, but at least they weren't saying he was completely wrong. Maybe his explanation wasn't a bad one after all, and Harry decided to act as if that was the case. *The game.* Adjusting his position, he prepared to observe the old man's act.

"By the way, Artie, have you thought any more about what you said yesterday? About my new name?"

"Ah, yes." Still looking worried, Arthur adjusted his tie as the lights sputtered out. "A fair number of magicians invent a new one. Something that catches the attention…"

"Had any more ideas?"

"I was doing some research earlier today, actually," Arthur continued. "Magicians sometimes name themselves after really famous magicians from long ago—that way they grab some of their reputation. Now there's this old French magician, very famous when he was alive, called Jean Robert-Houdin—"

"Quite a mouthful," Billie commented. "And Harry doesn't speak a word of French."

"Yes, but you could make it shorter. And change it a bit, so it's more like a name in Hungarian, which Harry obviously does speak. So *Houdin*. Stick an *i* on the end—*Houdini*."

"Interesting—" Harry began, but by then the curtain was rising. Prettily dressed ladies sang songs, acrobats tumbled, and Harry sat with his friends, watching the show. A new act followed, in which dancers pretended to be pearl divers, floating in front of a rippling blue backcloth as if under the sea. Harry enjoyed that too, even though he immediately spotted the wires that held the dancers up and saw that the huge shark was just a shadow.

The other acts trooped on—some Cossack dancers, a man who told jokes while dressed as a parrot, the pearl divers again, and then a leopard-skin-wearing strongman named Bruno, who made three of the prettily dressed ladies sit on a chair and then lifted it. *Another wire,* Harry observed. But then Herbie appeared and Harry leaned forward, concentrating.

The tiniest twitch of Herbie's trouser pocket, the faintest bulge of a sleeve, or the tilt of a shoe could give something away. Harry glanced down at his own hands, at his knees, at his whole body. Any minute now, bits of it would start twitching to life, practicing and mimicking whatever intriguing new move was about to be discovered.

"Ladies and gentlemen…" The old man bowed before the crowd. "Observe…"

From out of his jacket, he took a large knife. He quickly peeled a potato with it, proving the blade was razor-sharp. Then he tossed the knife high in the air, and as it plummeted back down, he held out a bare hand and caught it blade first between thumb and finger. No blood on the stage, no injury of any kind.

Dazzling enough, but then other knives started hurtling toward the old magician from the back of the theater, from the boxes, from the wings of the stage, only for Herbie to catch them, one by one, in his frail, bare hands. The audience gasped, and he held the knives aloft, looking up at their glinting steel. Harry leaned even further forward in his seat, searching for a clue.

But all he could see was that Herbie was trembling again. The old man had held it together during the trick, but now that the applause was thundering around him, he was giving way, his clothes shuddering, his wrinkles glittering in the light as perspiration coursed along them. Harry glanced at his friends and saw that they also had noticed, their faces staring worriedly in the dark.

It was like that for the rest of the act. Herbie performed his flower trick, in which not only did a flower grow out of his open hand, but a huge tropical spider scampered out, danced around the flower, and disappeared in a puff of smoke. Impossible to work out, but Harry wasn't even trying now, too distracted by the return of the trembling. Next the old man shut himself in a large crate. Although a large sack of stage weights plummeted onto the crate, crushing it flat, Herbie shuffled in from the wings unharmed.

Normally he walked in quite confidently, but there was no sign of that tonight. He seemed hardly able to walk at all, staying right at the edge of the stage and clinging to the proscenium arch for support. Finally, Herbie performed his floating trick, rising into the air and drifting off over a bed of vicious-looking spikes, while moving his legs as if he were pedaling a bicycle. But still Harry found it impossible to concentrate, too troubled by the terrible paleness of the old man's face as he cycled off into the gloom.

The curtain flew down. The audience clapped, hooted, and stamped. The curtain rose again, with the performers taking a bow, and then it lowered for good. The audience started shuffling out. But Harry remained in his seat, perfectly still, and Billie and Arthur were motionless beside him.

"I suppose you could be right about Herbie's behavior being a distraction, Harry," said Arthur after a while. "But it seems unlikely."

"Completely unlikely," said Billie.

"I agree," said Harry. What was up with Herbie? What was this strange weakness that seemed to be taking him over? Harry's fingers drummed on the rickety arms of the theater seat.

"Come on, we'll find him outside. He'll be leaving by the stage door."

"But that's against our agreement." Arthur looked uncertain. "He doesn't want us to meet him there. He's always said—"

"That's about us discovering his tricks! This is different—we're making sure he's all right! Come on!"

Harry sprang up, his shoeshine box flying up with him. He vaulted over the back of the seats, leaving Arthur and Billie floundering behind. Marching up the aisle toward the foyer doors, the only other member of the audience who had lingered behind.

A bulky figure, swathed in a dark cape. The man was hunched over a briefcase, an arm delving inside it. The face that glanced up at Harry had an oiled and curling red mustache, two piercing eyes, and a long, thin nose. On the collar of the cape, a silver brooch with a snake spiraled around a silver sword. From the briefcase, a wisp of purple smoke.

Odd. Harry's pace slowed. But Billie and Arthur were hurrying up the aisle behind him and slammed into his back. *Need to find Herbie*, Harry thought as he snatched his gaze away from the strange figure and swept on, out of the theater.

Chapter 5

"FOLLOW ME!" HARRY CALLED back.

"We're trying!" Billie sputtered.

"*Ow!*" Arthur gasped.

Harry ducked between people's legs in the crowd. A fair chunk of the audience was already bustling around the stage door. There was no chance of him being able to push his way through, so he had dropped to the ground and was crawling instead. Angling his shoeshine box through with him, he saw, farther back, his friends trying to follow. Arthur was tangled up in a lady's dress, while Billie was squashed between two heavy-looking suitcases.

"Stuck! This is like the Tennessee Stagecoach Squeeze! Bumped the whole journey on the stagecoach roof, jammed between two suitcases." Billie tried to pull herself loose. "I thought that was bad but—"

"Hurry, Billie!" Harry reached back, grabbed her

hand, and tugged. She lurched forward but then snagged her smock on a nearby boot's riding spur and got stuck again, while Arthur was still trying to free himself from the dress.

They'll catch up, thought Harry, and he wriggled onward until, at last, he popped out of the crowd, right by the stage door.

"The performers will be emerging soon! Autographs will be available—all included in the price of your ticket, naturally!" A plump gentleman with a flamboyant pink top hat squashed onto his head was bustling around in front of the crowd. Harry recognized him from his previous visits to the theater, when he had seen the man in the foyer welcoming the audience as they arrived—Mr. Wesley Jones himself. "What a show we had tonight—wouldn't you say, Arnold?"

"It was a swell 'un all right, Mr. Jones!" Loping after Wesley was a tall, gangly, wide-eyed young man, whose left leg dragged slightly behind him. Papers spilled out of a folder stuffed under his arm. "Herbie was powerful spectacular, I thought!"

"Ah, but he always is." Wesley snatched off the pink top hat. "Regarding Herbie, I'd pay close attention to Arnold if I were you, folks! He's my stage manager and he's seen the acts a thousand times. Why, he might have picked up a few clues about how old Herbie does his tricks!" The pink hat twirled between two thumbs. "Well, Arnold?"

"I don't know about that, Mr. Jones." The young man rearranged his papers, adjusted his left leg, and stood at attention as best he could. "Anyway, Herbie'll be down here soon enough. He's just up in his dressing room, taking a rest."

"Ah—but is he?" Another twirl of the hat, and Wesley winked over its rim. "Maybe, right at this very moment, he's up there carrying out preparation work for his next *incredible* trick. He never stops, y'know. He works on them endlessly…"

Intrigued cooing came from the crowd. Harry swung around and peered up at the rickety theater building. Seeing brightly lit windows running up the theater gave him an idea. He began wriggling back between the shoes, trouser legs, boots, and riding spurs, and nearly collided with Billie and Arthur, who were still only halfway through the crowd.

"Where are you going *now*?" Billie disentangled herself from an umbrella.

"Maybe it'll be easier, Billie!" Arthur was already trying to swivel around. "Going in the other direction, I mean."

It wasn't. It was much harder because the crowd was pushing toward the stage door, not away from it, and even Harry needed to wriggle with all his skill before he managed to tumble out onto the cobblestones. He sprang to his feet, crossed the street, and peered back up at the theater. And he saw exactly what he had hoped for.

In each of the theater windows, silhouettes of the various performers flitted as they changed out of their costumes. Two stories up, neatly framed in its window, was a silhouette that looked recognizably frail. *Herbie*. The old man was moving about, the shadows of his spindly arms fluttering in the light. Spotting a drainpipe running up the side of the theater, Harry ran across and started shimmying up.

"Harry? What are you doing?"

It was Arthur. He was staggering across the street, his tie crooked, his tweed suit a mess. Behind him, Billie scrambled up from the cobblestones with a puzzled expression on her face. They stumbled toward Harry, staring up at the window.

"There's Herbie!"

"I know! I'll climb up and see him. Who knows how long it'll be till he makes it down to the stage door? I know he doesn't want us inside the theater, but this isn't about tricks anymore!" Harry's arm shot up and pointed at various other drainpipes, window-sills, and gutters, a more-or-less possible route up the side of the theater. "Come on!"

They didn't look convinced. *Perhaps that's for the best*, thought Harry. A fair number of passersby were drifting along the street, so someone would be sure to notice three children clambering up the side of a theater. But alone and climbing with skill, he might make the journey undetected. Gripping one of the drainpipe's brackets, he continued shimmying up through the shadows.

"Harry! Look!"

"What's happening?"

Harry swung around. He saw Billie and Arthur, their arms pointing up at the window. Farther down the street, some of the passersby had stopped and also were staring up. Harry leaned out from the drainpipe, gazed up, and saw why.

The silhouette in Herbie's window was no longer just moving about. It was tripping, staggering. Not only that, but someone else seemed to have entered the dressing room. A shadow lurched into view, a thick, burly one, with arms lunging. Whoever it was, Herbie Lemster clearly wasn't happy to see them. The old man's spindly shape was flailing, trying to fend off the shadow, and Harry heard feeble muffled cries, followed by a louder, gruffer shout.

"What's yours is mine and always shall be! You remember that, Herbie Lemster!"

A flash of light. Harry's eyes throbbed with pain. An explosion thundered through the night, the drainpipe shuddered, and he lost his hold. He was falling, the explosion still shuddering as he plummeted. His arms and legs scrabbled about, thrashing at the air, and he slammed into the sidewalk, his body crumpling.

"Harry?"

He lay there. He felt the sting of the sidewalk's grit cutting deep into his hands, his knees, and the side of his head. He lurched to his feet. Stumbling forward, he found a lamppost and grabbed hold.

"Harry? Are you all right?"

"I'm fine…"

It was Billie. Her face peered at him. He saw Arthur coming toward him too. Harry stared at them, blinked, and then swung back to look at the window.

Its glass had been shattered. And corkscrewing out into the night sky…

…were plumes of thick, purple smoke.

Chapter 6

PURPLE WISPS DRIFTED DOWN from the window
and Harry choked on them, tasting chemicals
in his spit. His eyes still throbbed and his body ached
from the fall, but he kept stumbling on through the
plumes of smog, his gaze fixed on the crowd around
the stage door.

"Harry!" Arthur's voice was beside him. "Did you
see it?"

"Whole window blew out!" Billie appeared out of
the smoke, flapping at the fumes. "And look at all this
smoke! What the heck's going on, Harry—*Harry?*"

Help Herbie. Harry plunged into the crowd. It
was hysterical now, bodies shoving, legs intertwin-
ing. He thought of Herbie's strangely pale face
before the show. *And now, a thundering explosion, a
shattered window, a load of billowing purple smoke.*
The thoughts made him pick up speed, crawling,

diving through. Glancing back, he saw his friends, already hopelessly entangled. *They'll catch up*, he told himself again.

"Tell us what happened, Arnold! Speak to me!"

It was Wesley Jones. Harry toppled out between two boots and saw the theater owner, his pink top hat battered, crouching over the slumped shape of the stage manager. He was trying to sit the gangly young man up on the cobblestones, but Arnold's head kept lolling forward, and Harry saw that the stage manager had hit his head, blood trickling all the way down onto his shirt.

"I'd just gone inside, Mr. Jones, sir." Arnold was gasping. "Herbie was takin' so long, y'see."

"I know! I sent you!" Wesley swung around to face the crowd. "You all wanted to see Herbie. I couldn't keep you waiting any longer, could I?"

"So I went in, made my way up the stairs..." Arnold choked. "Then it happened, Mr. Jones. The flash of light! The smoke! I lost my balance, see...fell down the stairs..."

"And that's where I found him, ladies and gentlemen! At the foot of the stairs!" Wesley butted in. "He's always a little unsteady on his feet, poor guy. How on earth could he climb the stairs straight into a terrible explosion? To think of such a thing happening, in my theater of all places—"

"What about the intruder?" someone interrupted. It was one of the passersby who had watched the window from across the street. "We saw someone just before the explosion."

"Intruder?" Arnold's eyes sprang wide. "What are you talking about?"

"We saw him too!" Another voice from the crowd. "A shadow, but someone was there all right."

"He wasn't just there—he was attacking him! And what about the shout?"

"*What's yours is mine and always shall be!* That's what he said. I heard it, plain!"

"I heard it too!"

"But what does it mean—"

"An intruder in Herbie's dressing room?" Wesley butted in, his face white and wobbling. "But that makes the business even worse than I thought... You see, ladies and gentlemen, I was just about to tell you that..." He clutched his pink hat to his chest. "I managed to find my way to Herbie's dressing room in the end. I stumbled over Arnold here and climbed the stairs to make sure poor Herbie was all right," Wesley wailed. "But there was no sign of him, ladies and gentlemen. No sign at all! Herbie Lemster...he's *gone*!"

The crowd heaved forward. Harry barely managed to keep himself upright as the surging bodies carried him past Wesley, past Arnold, right into the theater itself. *A good thing*—maybe he could discover something that would tell him what was going on.

Backstage in the theater now and surrounded by pieces of scenery, he lodged himself between one of the enormous seaweed plants from the pearl-diving scene and a collection of ropes and iron hooks hung on the wall. He watched as the crowd swarmed.

"Intruder? But I saw no one!" It was Bruno the Strongman, still wearing his leopard skin, his muscles shaking. "I walked up to Herbie's dressing room with him after the show, like I do every night—there was no one in there with him then!"

"We didn't see anyone either!" One of the pearl-diving dancers spoke up, surrounded by a tight crowd of her friends, all in tears. "We were talking in the corridor. We saw Herbie go into his room and close the door—and that's all. No one visited. The door stayed shut. Until—boom! It knocked us all off our feet!"

"And no one came out of the dressing room after that. I swear it!" The man who told jokes was still dressed as a parrot, but the face among the feathers was pale and he didn't look like he'd say anything funny for quite some time. "I was at the very far end of the corridor just as it happened. It knocked me back, but I kept staring at Herbie's door. Sure, it blew open! Sure, there was smoke! But I'd have seen if anyone came out! Particularly if some intruder was tryin' to carry Herbie off against his will. I'd have seen it, I swear…"

Harry stumbled toward the nearby stairs. He joined the members of the crowd who were racing up them, pushing his way up one flight, then another, and along a corridor until he reached a door on which were painted the letters "H. Lemster." He toppled through and saw the shattered windows, some scorch marks on the rug, and a few wisps of purple smoke still hanging in the air. But his attention was fixed on one item in particular, leaning against the room's solitary chair.

Herbie's walking cane. The stick he had seen in his old friend's trembling hand less than an hour ago.

Harry started searching. His hands raced over the walls, checking for hidden doors or panels, and he crouched and inspected the floorboards. But there was nothing. He was sure of it, not least because everyone else was also searching. Countless hands raced over every inch of the room, finding nothing. Apart from the door to the corridor, the only other way out was the window, and he had been staring at that and would have seen if anyone tried to get out. What on earth had happened? Harry heard more shouts from outside the room and stumbled down to the theater's backstage.

"Poor Herbie! What has become of him?" one of the juggling acrobats asked. She was as upset as all the other performers who had gathered in a sobbing, mournful crowd.

"I'm afraid it's impossible to say." Wesley Jones wiped at tears with his bloodstained handkerchief. "Somehow, a mysterious intruder found his way into Herbie's dressing room. An explosion occurred, and the next thing we know, both Herbie and the intruder have vanished into thin air!"

"But who was this intruder? What would he want with ol' Herbie?" Arnold wheezed. "Herbie doesn't have an enemy in the world!"

"Never mind that—how did it happen?" A voice from the crowd, a slightly panicky one. "How did two men get out of the dressing room without anyone seeing them? Did they just disappear in a puff of smoke?"

"Maybe it was magic!" Another voice, more panicked still. "Maybe one of Herbie's tricks went wrong. He accidentally summoned this strange intruder and—"

"A demon!" This voice sounded positively hysterical. "Dark forces! That's what's behind this. Herbie Lemster has been claimed by his own magical powers!"

Pandemonium was breaking out. Harry was about to give up on hearing anything when one voice managed to cut through, louder, more hysterical than any other.

"Magic? Dark forces? I've no idea!" It was Wesley Jones. "Only one thing is clear, and it's this: ladies and gentlemen, I regret to confirm to you that"—his voice broke with a sob but kept going—"Herbert Lemster, marvelous magician, has…*disappeared*!"

The pandemonium was complete, the screams blotting each other out. It was impossible to hear anything, and it was becoming impossible to see anything either because the crowd was swarming too fast, too tightly, Wesley and Arnold trying to keep control in the middle. Harry fought his way out. Ducking through the bodies and pushing out through the stage door, he hurried across the street, breathing in the cool night air.

He found a lamppost and steadied himself against it, his hand gripping the iron. He breathed more deeply. The purple smoke had drifted away, so the air was clear, and its coldness was useful too. Harry stood there, sucking in lungful of it as he thought through everything he had discovered about this business so far—and about one piece of information in particular.

The man he had seen just a short time ago as he walked up the theater's aisle.

"Harry! What's going on?"

He saw Billie and Arthur racing after him, even as he marched along the street, swung around the corner, and headed toward the theater's front doors. Had they been backstage in the theater too, somewhere in the crowd? Or had they been out here the whole time, waiting? Harry lifted an arm and waved his friends after him.

"Come on! We've got to hurry!"

"Huh?" Billie hurried after him. "What's happened to Herbie?"

"Tell us!" Arthur cried. "What did you find out?"

"I've got to check something." Harry slammed through the doors, straight into the deserted foyer. Almost immediately, his friends slammed through after him.

"Check what? Slow down, will you?"

"The man we saw…the one with the briefcase…" Into the auditorium and down the aisle. "Maybe there's some trace of it left behind…some clue…"

"Man? Briefcase? What are you talking about?"

"I'll explain everything. Just let me…"

He turned and stared at a particular seat. He lunged toward it, and his hands explored its back, its arms, and the floor around it, searching for anything that might have been left behind. Nothing could be seen, but Harry felt his nostrils twitch as he leaned close to the seat's left arm. He sniffed the arm's worn upholstery. Faintly, very faintly, he could detect the same chemical odor of the purple smoke that had billowed outside.

"Er…Harry? What are you doing?"

"Since when did you start sniffing chairs?"

Harry looked up. The expression on Arthur's face was very puzzled, and the corner of Billie's mouth had curved into a smile. Harry stood up, straightened his jacket, and pointed at the chair.

"The man who was sitting right there. He's our only clue."

And he told them. He told them about those piercing eyes. He told them about the oiled, red mustache and how its ends had curled upward. As his words raced out, he found himself remembering other details—the brooch on the cape, the sinister snake coiled around an upright sword—and he told them about those as well. Finally, he told them about the most important, most sinister detail of all.

The man's briefcase.

Out of which had spiraled that tiny wisp of purple smoke.

Chapter 7

HARRY WOKE UP.

He lay there, listening to the sounds of Mrs. Mack's boarding house coming to life—the coughs and murmurings of the other lodgers, the scrape of chairs. His nose twitched as he breathed in the smell of Mrs. Mack's gruel, which he had long ago learned to avoid. Looking up, he saw beads of morning light sliding through the broken roof tiles over his head. He lifted his hand and let the sun play over it, slanting between his fingers, surrounding them.

Flexing his fingers, he tried to move them through the crisscrossing rays without them being touched, and succeeded, apart from a single spot of light just glancing off his thumb. It was a game he had invented back in the slums of Budapest, his faraway Hungarian home, where the roof over his bed had also been broken. He had played it ever since, and he played it now.

His fingers crept through the light. The smell of the gruel sweetened into the warm fragrance of *zsemle*, the buns his mother used to bake every morning. He breathed the scent in and heard, very faintly, the whispering of his father reciting prayers as the family sat by the fire. Harry's fingers crept on as the sweet smells and whispers drifted around him, and then, all at once, disappeared.

He saw his parents' faces—fearful and tightly drawn. He heard his father's words, but they weren't prayers now. They were frightened mutterings, talk of money and debts, which Harry hadn't understood back then, and which seemed even murkier as he tried to recall them now. But he had understood what happened next. "The Scattering," they had called it.

The family had broken up, his father sending them off across Europe to wherever there might be hope for them, which in Harry's case had meant ending up in the hold of a ship sailing across the Atlantic. Four weeks the voyage had lasted, four weeks of filth, hunger, and sickness. But even so, nothing had prepared him for his arrival in New York and his new life as a shoeshine boy in this cold, hard city where he knew no one.

Harry stared up at his fingers flashing in the light. *These skills*, he thought, *they are what changed everything*. Without them, he would still be that shoeshine boy, nothing more. Without them, he would never have met Billie and Arthur, the two best friends he had ever had. Yes, life in New York would have been grim indeed, he thought, if he hadn't picked up these extraordinary tricks.

And that was all thanks to Herbie Lemster.

Harry sprang up and slid his feet into his boots. A splash of water and he clattered down the rickety stairs and pushed past the shadows of the other lodgers rising from their beds—laborers, travelers, ne'er-do-wells. Passing a murky mirror by the stairs, he glimpsed himself and saw smudges of shoe polish on his face. But there was no time to rub it clean, not this morning.

Help Herbie.

He shot out through the rickety front door. Heading off through the Manhattan streets, he swung west to Grand Central Station, where men of business were pouring off the morning trains. Here Harry quickly did a couple polishing jobs, crouching over the proffered shoes, wiping them clean, and shining them up. The cold sidewalk hurt his knees and the polish stung his fingers, but he reminded himself he needed to eat to be able to concentrate—today of all days—and so he kept shining until enough coins had dropped into his palm.

Then he hurried to a pastry stall, handed the money over, and stuffed a pie into his mouth. Gathering up any pastry flakes that dangled on his clothes, he ate them too and walked away from the station. He threaded through some alleys, crossed a market square, slanted along another alley, and arrived at a large hulking factory with gray fumes spooling from it.

"Mawkin's Glue Factory," a sign said on the front. Harry checked a clock in a nearby shop window and ran to the factory's front door, which was firmly locked. He listened and could make out raised voices on the other side, one deep and growling, the other high-pitched and familiar. *Billie.* The voices grew louder, and something smashed—*Time to carry out the plan.*

Harry hurried around the back of the factory. Spotting a hay cart on the nearby cobblestones, he tugged it across to the factory wall and, with a quick swivel, positioned it correctly. Hearing scrabbling sounds from the other side of the wall, he propped an arm against the cart and tried to look casual in case anyone should pass by, but already something was blurring over the wall's top. The cart wobbled, bits of hay flew, and Billie landed right in front of him, even more spattered with glue than usual. That deep voice bellowed from inside the factory, but already racing off with his friend down the alley, Harry couldn't make out the words.

"Guess that's it for the whole 'stirring gray gloop for two cents an hour' racket." Billie tossed her cap into a bin. "Can't say I mind."

"You asked him for the day off, I guess." Harry glanced back.

"Asked him at eight o'clock exactly, just like we agreed. And obviously he said no. Not even when I said it was an emergency, which helping poor Herbie most surely is. Said it was his right to make me work the rest of the day, in return for having given me paid work and a bed for so long! And when I told him his pay was nothing and his bed stank of poisonous glue—well, that's when he started chasing me with the broom. So I decided to go for our little plan and ran for the back wall, tipping a pot of slippery boiled-up bones in his path as I went." She jerked a thumb back toward the factory, which was already far behind. "Crummy job."

"Crummier than all the others?" Harry asked.

"Well now, that's a good question." Billie slowed down and a frown appeared on her face, just for a few seconds. "It's true, I've ended up doing a fair number of tough jobs on the way up from New Orleans. Cleaning drains, sweeping floors, picking through garbage heaps, you name it." She looked back again.

"Can't say that was the crummiest boss I've had or the first broom I've had to dodge. Still, it's not the sticky situations you get into; it's how you get out of them, that's what I say." She shrugged and ducked around a corner. "Somehow or other, I've managed to get myself unstuck—one way or another. Why, I even managed to get unstuck from a glue factory, didn't I?" Her smile was back. "Not a bad escape. The Glue Pot Scramble, that's what I'll call it. You did well with that cart business too."

"Thanks, Billie."

"Sort of makes up for you being so crazy last night."

Harry felt his face grow warm, even though they were no longer running, just walking along. He looked away and tried to think of different ways of putting it but decided in the end just to say what he had before.

"I'm sorry. I just needed to help Herbie—couldn't think of anything apart from that. And it happens sometimes, you know that. When I—"

"Get swept up in stuff, can't think of anything else. It's how you do your tricks. I know, I know." Billie speeded up, burst out of the alley, and looked around. "The thing is, this isn't just a trick, is it? It's way more important than that! And we're all friends with Herbie, so we're in this together, yeah?"

"Of course." Harry's pace quickened.

"Anyway, there's Artie. Come on!"

She jumped over some railings and ran across the park. The bright white house towered nearby, and Harry followed Billie to the same rhododendron bush as the day before. Waiting behind it stood Artie, his pocket watch ticking in his hand. He looked up at them, jerked his head toward the house, and nodded.

"Thanks, guys. Head over there now. You'll be right on time."

Harry and Billie set off. They left the park, crossed the street, and reached the sidewalk just as the front door of Arthur's house opened. A servant trod down the stone steps. He wasn't as tall as Lord Trilby-Roberts but every bit as stiff and with a stare every bit as cold. That stare was fixed on the small iron mailbox a few yards down the sidewalk, and he headed toward it, a collection of letters fluttering in his hand. But he never managed to deliver them because Harry had let himself be pushed by Billie, straight into the servant's path.

"Watch out!"

Harry toppled into the servant. The letters flew everywhere, but Harry snatched them out of the air and, with a swoop of his arm, helpfully posted them in the mailbox.

"Ever so sorry, sir! My friend, she's always doing that… Come back here!"

He ran after Billie before the servant could reply. But a flash of his hand had done the trick. As the letters spun in the air, he had spotted one with a particular address, and it had slid into his jacket as the others vanished into the mailbox. It rustled there now as he followed Billie down the street, back into the park, and behind a tree. They waited until the servant had vanished back into the house and slid across to the rhododendron bush again.

"Nice work," Arthur said, taking the letter.

"We just did the snatch." Harry shrugged as they walked off. "How'd you know the servants would be posting the letter to the school at that exact moment?"

"Father gave them instructions yesterday, and they always act immediately. They always post the day's mail at ten o'clock, so it stood to reason the letter to the school would be in with it." He turned and looked back at the house. "Father left for Chicago at dawn, by the way. Obviously, he didn't bother to say good-bye."

Arthur's eyes narrowed again. His jaw clenched, and a row of teeth bit down hard on his lower lip. Harry glanced at Billie, worried again. Artie tapped the letter in his hands, swung around, and kept marching away.

"So what's the next step, Artie?" Billie asked as they walked out through the park gates and cut across the street. "We've got the letter, but how are we going to keep you from ending up at this boarding school? Bad enough, your father acting like you don't exist, but we definitely can't have him sending you 452 miles away. How are Harry and I supposed to cope without our best pal?"

"It's all right, Billie." Arthur slid the letter into his jacket pocket. "Now that I've got this, it'll all be easy. I've been borrowing books from the library about forgery, copying signatures, that sort of thing. All that research will come in useful now."

"You're going to write to the school calling the whole thing off?" wondered Harry.

"Cleverer than that." Arthur led them around a

corner. "Look, I'll let you know how it goes, but don't worry—I'm staying around."

"That's good," said Harry. "I agree with Billie—we don't want you disappearing anywhere, especially now there's this stuff with Herbie to sort out."

"I'm glad you feel that way, Harry," said Arthur. "After the way you were last night, I wasn't so sure."

For the second time, Harry felt his face grow warm. Arthur had turned away, so Harry couldn't quite see his expression, but his friends were talking about something—he could hear their mutterings even if he couldn't quite make out the words. *Think of something to say, something that will make it better*, he told himself, and he tried to do just that, but it was difficult, and it grew even more difficult the nearer they came to the destination where they would start work on their vital task. Hadn't Billie herself said, just a few minutes ago, that nothing mattered more than that? Harry thought again of that left-behind walking cane in the dressing room, surrounded by a few wisps of purple smoke.

"It's all right, Harry. I know you didn't mean it." Arthur tugged his friend's sleeve and swerved to the left. "Anyway, it's time to get started."

They walked a few blocks, and then across the street

was the New York Library. Pillars towered at the top of wide marble steps, and Arthur led Harry and Billie up them, through a pair of huge bronze doors, and into the enormous entrance hall. It dwarfed his tiny tweed-suited figure, but there was something impressive about the speed with which he marched across the hall, his fingers clicking at his sides, his tie flapping over his shoulder.

"I dropped in here earlier actually, checked a few things, made a good start. But I'm going to need you to draw that mustache again, Harry."

"No problem, Artie." Harry followed his friend.

"The snake and sword design too. Maybe you'll remember something else about it this morning. Every detail counts if we're to find out who he is…"

Arthur led them into the reading room, with its high windows and hunched figures scribbling at desks. A swerve to the left and he pushed through a door. Scampering down a corkscrewing staircase, he led them to the library's musty basement and started weaving his way through its maze of corridors, each one lined with thousands of books. Fingers still clicking, he didn't hesitate even slightly as he found his way through.

"You sure do know this library well, Artie," said Harry.

"Certainly spent enough time here. Remember, before I met you guys, there wasn't exactly much else for me to do." His voice had gone quiet. Harry peered at him in the gloom and knew that the quietness had nothing to do with the various signs saying "Silence" and hanging nearby. "Anyway, who cares about that? We're here."

"I'll get drawing," said Harry.

They were at the end of the corridor. A desk stood covered with carefully stacked piles of books and papers, and Harry immediately sat down at it. Pinned to the wall behind were the various drawings that he had sketched for Arthur the previous night, different attempts at the curling mustache and silver brooch. Immediately, he grabbed a fresh sheet of paper and a pencil, and started drawing again.

Nearby, Arthur climbed a wheeled ladder and started leafing through books on a high shelf. Billie pushed the ladder along so that he could make his way through them at high speed. Harry worked away, trying to remember what he had seen with even more care. Once the drawings were done, he held them up. Billie was beside him immediately, snatching them out of his hand and springing up the ladder with them.

"Useful," said Arthur, studying the sketches. "I'm definitely onto something."

Clever stuff, thought Harry, watching his friend tear through books at an even greater speed. It was one thing to be able to spot so many details—and another to know what to do with those details. Billie was hard at work too, leaping up and down that ladder, and transporting tottering piles of books back to the desk. Sitting back, Harry gripped the pencil in his fist and wondered if there was anything else he could draw.

The face itself? But that would be much harder than simply drawing a mustache or a snake. It would take a highly experienced artist to capture the glimmer of those eyes, the shadowiness of those features, the cruelness of that mouth, all of which had combined to make that face so unsettling. Who was that sinister, bulky figure? Harry's grip on the pencil tightened as he thought back to that exact moment, halfway up the aisle, when he had noticed the wisp of smoke and looked up to see that piercing gaze...

"We're just getting started." Billie was taking a break, sitting cross-legged on the table, her boots propped on the edge of Harry's chair. "It's one thing to work out who he is. But then we'll have to figure out *where* he might be—he could be anywhere in New York by now!"

"There'll be a way." Harry looked up at the blur of tweed-suited arms and fluttering pages high on the wheeled ladder. "We just need to let Artie do his stuff."

"Sure, sure." Billie's boots swapped places. "But there's an even bigger thing to figure out—and that's *why*. Some guy breaks into Herbie's dressing room and makes off with him in a puff of purple smoke—why'd he do that?"

"That's what no one knows." Harry lifted the pencil to his mouth and gnawed at its end. "Herbie doesn't have an enemy in the world. They said that over and over again."

"Doesn't have an enemy in the world that anyone's *heard of*. But if you've got an enemy, you're not likely to go around telling people, are you? Might be safer to keep it quiet." Billie frowned. "I've been thinkin' and thinkin', Harry. Did Herbie ever say anything to us that might be some sort of clue? Something about his past?"

"I've been thinking too." Harry took the pencil from his mouth. "If only we'd tried to talk to him yesterday. Asked him why he was acting so odd. He'd have let something slip. I'm sure of it."

"I've got something," said Arthur, thudding a book onto the desk.

Gentlemen's Fashion in Eastern Europe. Harry lifted the cover and flicked through a few pages. Various inked drawings of hats and coats. Not what Harry had expected—but Arthur was already explaining.

"So I started with the mustache. Mustache styles are totally different the world over. As soon as you described this one to me, I knew it wasn't from anyone brought up around here. I fetched out a load of books on fashion and barbering, and flicked though. Made a list of likely contenders and, once I had your sketch, went for the closest match. Turns out this curled, oiled style is fashionable among men in their fifties from Bulgaria, Eastern Europe." He riffled through the book and planted a finger on a page. "Is this the mustache you saw last night?"

There it was, the same mustache, neatly illustrated. *Impressive*—and already Arthur was hurrying back up the ladder and stumbling down it again with a new pile of books.

"So the fact that he's a Bulgarian doesn't get us very far on its own. But then there's the snake-and-sword brooch, and that's what I worked on next. It could just be a decoration obviously. But that's unusual for men—generally, if they wear a brooch or badge, it's because they're part of some sort of organization and that's the emblem.

"Now, there are a lot of societies and organizations in the world, but ones with snakes or swords for an emblem are rare. Bulgaria narrows it down even more. I'm pretty quick at flicking through books, plus your drawings are dead accurate, Harry, particularly the one you did just now." Another open book thudded onto the table. "The badge you saw last night is worn by members of this society, based in Gabrovo, Bulgaria."

Halfway down the page, a snake coiled around a sword—exactly the same as the one on the lapel the previous night.

"The society's official title is the Grand Gabrovo Order of Magical Illusionists."

A magicians' society. Harry studied the snake. Its coils were intricate and unfathomable, just like the mystery they were trying to solve. But out of those coils, the snake's head glared clearly, and out of the mystery, a single piece of information was glaring at him too. The man in the theater was a magician.

Makes sense, thought Harry. Who else would be able to pull off a trick like making an old man disappear from his dressing room in a puff of smoke? *A magician, and a sinister one at that.* Those memories flickered again, of Herbie's fear, of those telltale trembling signs. Harry kept staring at the snake, noticing how it curled around the sword. That wisp of smoke had curled too, in a way that was every bit as unnerving. But most unnerving of all had been that face, with its glittering eyes and its long, thin nose—long and thin as the blade of a knife…

"Er, Harry?"

Harry looked up. Perhaps his friends were also thinking troubling thoughts. Their eyes were wide open, their faces even a little pale.

"I think we've discovered something else about that guy you saw, Harry," whispered Billie, pointing a finger down the corridor.

"What?" Harry turned…

"He's standing right there!"

Chapter 8

THE SINISTER MAGICIAN. THE shadowy shape of the bulky figure could just be seen, framed in the doorway at the corridor's far end. A scrawny library assistant hovered next to him, which only made the magician seem more enormous. A black cape swept down from his bulky shoulders, two huge fists hung at his sides, and those eyes glittered in the corridor's gloom. But so far, he hadn't looked down the corridor. He was too busy, stooped over the librarian and muttering. There was still time.

No sudden moves. A panicky leap would cause that huge head to swivel, those eyes to glint. Harry glanced at his friends on either side of him and decided not to take any chances. His hands shot out, and he grabbed Arthur and Billie. With a single, well-judged step, he pulled them silently back into the shadows behind them, which were just dark enough to provide cover.

Just like a trick. Arthur gaped, and Billie sputtered as if about to say something. Harry's hands rose again, covering his friends' mouths. He kept moving, guiding his friends stealthily back through the shadows until they reached the doorway at the other end of the corridor.

"Will that be all, Mr. Zell?"

So that was his name. After the librarian's nervous mutter drifted through the gloom, Harry peered back through the doorway. But only by the tiniest amount, because Zell was moving down the corridor now. Dismissing the librarian with a wave of his hand, the huge magician strode toward the table at the corridor's side where Harry and his friends had been working. He reached it and picked up one of the books that lay there, open at the page with the drawing of the snake and the sword. The magician's eyes stared at it, then flicked about the corridor even more keenly.

Billie pushed Harry's hand away from her mouth. "What's he doing here?"

"It just doesn't make sense!" A muffled hiss from Arthur.

"We only bumped into him for a second, didn't we?"

"So how come he knows we're here?"

"I don't know…" whispered Harry. "I don't… *Watch out!*"

Zell had heard them talking. The huge head snapped around, those eyes glittering straight at the doorway. Harry grabbed his friends' arms, tugging them off down the corridor so fast that the books on the shelves blurred into one brown smear. Together, they slammed into a spiral staircase, corkscrewed up it, and slanted down another corridor, racing through the gloom.

"He'll head for the main entrance," Harry gasped. "That's the obvious way to get out. He'll wait for us there, so we need to get out someplace else—any ideas, Artie?"

"Not really. I know the library pretty well, but I've never tried to *escape* from it before—"

"A door that leads outside! A window, anything! There's got to be one!"

"Hang on…" Arthur scratched his head as they raced along. "I think I might have seen some sort of service entrance, over on the west side."

"Show us!"

Harry pushed his friend on ahead. Several more corridors, another spiral staircase, endless shelves of books, and they finally arrived at an iron door in the library's west wall. Billie grabbed its handle and pulled.

"Locked!"

"Don't worry!" Harry was already running back along the corridor.

"Don't worry? What do you mean?"

Harry checked the books on the shelves and found one with a couple of notes attached to it by a paper clip. Removing the clip, he ran back to the door, peered through the keyhole, and started bending that little length of wire into a curve.

"Been practicing, haven't I. Any bit of stray metal can be a pick, just have to bend it right for the lock." He gave the clip a final tweak and slid it in. "Bent the nail for the padlock yesterday, and I had to use my mouth to pick that lock. Using your hands makes it easier and—"

A click, a ping, and they were out in the pale September light. A short flight of steps led down to the cobbled street that ran along the library's north side. Harry and his friends toppled down the stairs, their eyes adjusting to the brightness after the library's gloom.

"I just don't get it!" Billie brushed the sleeve of her smock where Harry had grabbed her. "How could he possibly know we would be at the library?"

"Maybe he's been following us!" Arthur was straightening his clothes too.

"But why?" sputtered Billie. "Why would he follow three kids? And how could he have done it? I'd have spotted anyone snooping after me, you bet I would!"

"He's a magician. He can probably do all kinds of things." Arthur swung around. "I say, Harry—you don't think he might actually have *real* magic powers, do you?"

"Now that would explain it!" gasped Billie. "There we are investigating him, and he pops up out of nowhere... Were there any wisps of purple smoke around him just now, Harry? Harry?"

Harry said nothing. His heart was pounding after the run though the library, but his head was pounding too. He lifted his fingers to it. It was as if he could feel the quivering of so many thoughts flying around inside. Zell, that was the magician's name, and he was a member of some kind of magicians' society in Bulgaria. But what was he doing here in New York? Why was he so interested in Herbie? How had he managed, magician or not, to make the poor old man vanish from his dressing room, leaving no trace at all...

"There he is!"

Billie and Arthur were up ahead, peering around the corner of the library. Harry joined them and peered too. They had been absolutely right not to head for the library's main doors because Zell was bursting out through them, that bulky head sweeping from side to side as he glanced around. But he clearly couldn't see them because after a few more glances, he strode down the library's marble steps toward a horse-drawn cab that was wheeling around to meet him.

A few muttered words to the driver, and he lurched inside, the whole vehicle tilting with his weight. The driver's whip cracked, the horses' hooves flung themselves against the cobblestones, and the cab rattled off. *Need to be quick*, thought Harry, and he leaped off the curb, his eyes flicking around as he tried to work out the best way to give chase.

"Let's get a cab too." Arthur pulled open the door of a nearby carriage. "I'll pay."

"To Hotel Crosby, please," Billie said to the driver of the cab that had just pulled up. Arthur jumped inside, and she followed, tugging Harry in after her.

"But…Hotel Crosby? Where's that? How do you know it's where he's going?" Harry bounced around on the seat as their cab rattled away.

"Easy," said Billie. "I lip-read what Zell said to the driver. Guess I never told you the story of Sherman

Jones, the tramp I bumped into when things were truly tough back on the road, down Virginia way? Sherman couldn't hear, but he could lip-read perfectly, and he taught me how to do it too. It's amazing what you can do if you can work out what people are saying without them knowing—explains my brief career as a mind reader at a fairground."

She laughed. "We were a good team, me and Sherman. Almost as good as the three of us right now." She looked at Arthur and then, quite suddenly, at Harry. "That was a pretty good stunt we pulled off back there, don't you reckon?"

Sure was, thought Harry. And it was going to take many more stunts, every bit as good, if they were going to see this matter through. Three times he had spotted Zell now, and on each occasion he had seemed every bit as threatening as the time before. What was this menacing figure's business with poor Herbie? Harry's whole body flinched at the thought. He wound down the cab window and stared out. Down at the far end of the street, he saw Zell's cab wheel to a halt outside a tall, drab building about ten stories high. "The Hotel Crosby," a sign said.

Zell stepped down onto the sidewalk, marched straight up the hotel's steps, and vanished through some revolving doors, a blur of glass and bronze. Once their cab stopped, Harry swung out through the door onto the sidewalk and peered toward the hotel. He focused in particular on the hotel's doorman standing right beside the doors, a thick-set fellow wearing a grubby top hat and coat, his arms folded behind his back and his eyes flicking up and down the street in an unfriendly way.

"How are we going to get past *him*?" muttered Arthur as he and Billie joined Harry. "Mean-looking fellow."

"You bet he is," said Billie. "But we managed to track Zell down somehow or other, so we'll get into his hotel too. Let's get thinking, Artie." She started pacing back and forth. "How about… What if…?"

"Can I borrow your ukulele, Billie?"

"What?"

The idea had hit Harry all at once. The plan for getting into the hotel had simply turned up, perfectly thought through. There were risks, plenty of them, but nothing he couldn't deal with, so he decided to put the plan into action right away. *It's not like Billie's actually come up with a plan of her own yet.* If she had, she would certainly say so. He knew that, but instead she just looked at him in an increasingly baffled way as he pulled her ukulele off her shoulder and started untuning the strings.

"Harry?"

"A distraction, that's all we need. Just like one of my tricks! If you want people to not see something, you just give them something else to look at. You wave a flower or a handkerchief or something, and while they're busy looking at that—"

"You're not going in without us, are you?"

It was Arthur who had spoken. Harry looked up and saw a troubled expression on his friend's face. Next to him, Billie was frowning, her arms crossed. While still fiddling with the ukulele's keys, Harry tried to explain.

"Look, we've got to help Herbie. That's what matters. Remember what we said, Artie—the three of us would never have even met if it hadn't been for Herbie Lemster! Well, he needs our help now, and I think we should give it to him anyway we can."

"That's true." The look was still on Arthur's face, troubled and puzzled. "It's just that normally the three of us work together. You, me, and Billie. We listen to each other, talk things through, and—"

"We will be working together! We'll just be working on different things, that's all. You'll do the distracting and I'll go in—"

A final twang. The ukulele was out of tune. *They'll come around once they hear the plan,* Harry told himself.

And he started telling his friends what he needed them to do.

Chapter 9

H ARRY HID IN THE alley. The wall behind him was damp, unpleasant smells drifted up from the ground, and a rat crept past one of his boots. But he let none of that distract him. *Just like a trick*—the slightest hesitation or fumble would lead to disaster. *But there won't be any hesitations or fumbles*, he told himself as he peered across the street.

Drifting along it was a discordant twanging. Arthur, looking a bit nervous, was hesitantly strumming the ukulele just outside the Hotel Crosby. Harry had carefully chosen him, not Billie, for the task, asking him to attempt one of Billie's most complicated songs—a ballad about a cowboy trying to cross the Mississippi River—and knowing the results would be particularly awful. Billie was part of the plan as well, and by now she would have taken up her position.

"You stop that din! You stop it now!"

The doorman was shaking his fist. As they came down the marble steps, a few of the hotel's guests were looking at the tweed-suited, ukulele-twanging boy, one lady even covering her ears, and the doorman had had enough. He was stomping down the steps, his fist still raised, his voice bellowing in Arthur's direction.

"Scram! You hear?"

Arthur scrammed. He ran as fast as he could, but the doorman was nearly upon him and would easily have grabbed Arthur if the garbage can by the nearby railings had not toppled forward. *Perfect.* Crouched behind the metal can, Billie had done her bit, kicking it forward at just the right time. The doorman stumbled straight into it, his fist flailing after the fleeing Arthur. He didn't even see Billie as she darted away from the railing in the opposite direction.

And he definitely won't see me, thought Harry as he flew up the marble steps and slid through the revolving doors. As they spun him around, he peered through, made out what he needed, and decided his next move. Stepping out into the lobby, he lunged sideways. A couple of porters pushed a luggage cart, and a clerk was working at the reception counter, but no one saw him because he was safely behind the large aspidistra plant to the left of the doors. Not one of the plant's leaves was even slightly trembling—*nicely done*.

The clerk stood up from the counter and was heading across the lobby toward a pair of double doors as Harry slid out from the aspidistra, hurried across the hall, and glided behind the counter. Grabbing the hotel guest book, he bundled himself into a cupboard.

He pulled the door almost shut, leaving a tiny shaft of light to spill onto the pages as he turned them. The names of all the hotel's guests were written there, along with their room numbers and the date they had signed in. His finger slid down the list, but he didn't recognize any names. Then his finger stopped, halfway down the ledger's second page.

"Boris Zell. Arrived September fourteenth. Room 760."

So there he was. Boris Zell, that was his full name. Boris Zell, who was a member of the Grand Gabrovo Order of Magical Illusionists. Boris Zell, who had been seen at the theater. Boris Zell, who had uncannily turned up at the library just now—so uncannily that Arthur and Billie, with some fairness, had put it down to actual magical powers. Harry closed the ledger, slid out of the cupboard, and rummaged about the counter, searching for any possible clue about the guest in Room 760.

His hands flew around, finding nothing. But there was a door near the counter on which was written "Manager's Office," so he decided to try that. He pushed at the handle and found it was locked. Another pick was needed and his other hand was already reaching back toward something he had spotted on the counter, a dirty fork and plate, the remains of the reception clerk's breakfast. *Perfect*. Harry grabbed the fork, wiped it on his sleeve, bent back three of its prongs, peered into the lock's keyhole, and curved the fourth prong until it was exactly the right shape. He pushed the prong into the keyhole, angled it upward, and...

The lock sprang open. Harry bent back the prongs and replaced the fork neatly on the plate. Then he slid into the manager's office and immediately noticed the day's mail, a knotted bundle on the manager's desk. He undid it and riffled through the letters. Two of them were for Mr. Boris Zell, both in Bulgarian, which Harry didn't understand, so he tossed them aside. But filed with them was a telegram in English, addressed to Boris too. Harry lifted it up and read it carefully.

• TELEGRAM •

TO: MR. BORIS ZELL C/O HOTEL CROSBY, NY

FROM: MR. OSCAR MUNTZ, MANAGER, VARIETY
THEATER, CHICAGO

WE CONFIRM BOOKING OF YOUR ACT FOR
EVENING OCTOBER 1ST 1886. WE NOTE YOU
CLAIM YOUR ACT WILL CONTAIN CERTAIN
NEW TRICKS, ENTITLED: BICYCLING OVER
SPIKES, THE FLYING KNIVES, AND SPIDER
UP SLEEVE. WE WILL ADVERTISE SUCH
TRICKS AND THEREFORE INSIST YOU
PERFORM THEM OR NO FEE PAYABLE.

Just a single sheet of paper that would have cost twenty cents to send, no more. But this was without question a very important discovery, and an unsettling one too. Harry dropped into a nearby chair to take it all in. *Why would anyone want to make off with poor Herbie in the first place?* Here, resting in his hand, was a possible and very unpleasant answer to Billie's question.

The game, Herbie had called it. Magicians studied

other magicians, seeking to uncover the secrets to each other's tricks. This had been going on for more than a thousand years, Herbie had said. But what if one magician chose to take the game a little too far? What if a magician tried to get hold of the secret to some tricks, not simply by watching...but by any means he could?

"Poor Herbie," Harry muttered.

The telegram proved it. It was clearly a reply to one Boris had sent earlier, seeking a booking for his show. Nothing wrong with that—except for the list of acts Boris was offering. They were Herbie's tricks. "Bicycling over Spikes" must refer to the one in which Herbie floated effortlessly over the bed of spikes as if riding a bicycle, and "The Flying Knives" and "Spider up Sleeve" were Herbie's too. Boris was promising to perform Herbie's tricks—yet how could he do that if he didn't know their secrets? So that was the telegram. But what about the shout that had been heard that night?

"What's yours is mine and always shall be!"

Herbie hadn't just disappeared. He had been kidnapped. Boris had snatched him from his dressing room—and if the Bulgarian was ruthless enough to do that, what might he be doing now? Would he have imprisoned Herbie somewhere, starving him until he gave up what he knew? Or did he have other devices, as mysterious and sinister as his purple smoke, with which he could persuade the old man to blurt out his dearly kept secrets...?

The office door was opening. Sunk in the chair, Harry had almost forgotten where he was. Stuffing the telegram into his pocket, he leaped up and rolled under the desk as the hotel manager, a short, bustling man, rushed in. Fortunately, he left the door open behind him, so Harry was able to slide out to the safety of the reception counter. *I'll break into Room 760*, he decided. In there, he would discover clues to how Boris had performed this kidnapping, where he might have hidden poor Herbie, and more besides.

But for now, he just needed to get out from behind the counter. Peering over it, he made out the porters and some guests. No one was looking directly toward him, so he made a dash for it, sliding across the marble floor toward the aspidistra. *Perfectly timed*, he thought, and then he saw something and realized he was much, much too late.

A bulky figure was striding across the lobby. A dark cape swept down to his shoes; a dark hat tipped over his face. The figure stopped and looked straight at Harry, who was still several feet away from the plant.

It was Boris Zell.

Chapter 10

THOSE CRUEL EYES GLITTERED. A lip flexed, and above it, the oiled mustache curled. On the dark cape, the snake-and-sword brooch gleamed. Worst of all, as Harry skidded toward the aspidistra, the telegram rustled in his pocket, evidence of Boris Zell's utterly ruthless plan.

Ruthless regarding Herbie, Harry thought. *And probably just as bad for anyone who tried to help him.*

"You! You were there…" Those piercing eyes narrowed. "Last night at the theater…I saw you!"

The face darkened. Nostrils flared. Harry decided not to hang around. Besides, the bustling hotel manager had just slammed out of his office and was pointing a finger straight at Harry.

"He's been in my office! Gone through the post and everything! Stolen something too, I'd say. Catch him quick!"

Harry dived past Zell. He tried to reach the revolving doors but found himself staring at the doorman, who was marching back in. Harry struck off across the lobby instead, but everywhere he looked, porters, clerks, and even some of the guests were running toward him. He threw himself through a pair of double doors. His boots pounded down a corridor, voices bellowing behind him.

"Stop him!"

"Thief!"

His boots pounded on, and his heart pounded even faster. On he raced, toward more double doors. He risked a glance behind him—his pursuers were getting closer. He slammed through the doors. Darting to the left, he burst into a stairwell and raced up three flights of stairs, his pursuers' cries spiraling up after him.

"We've got him now!"

"Block off the other staircase!"

"He can't keep going up forever!"

More doors. Another corridor, on the hotel's third floor. Windows ran along one side of it, and as Harry flashed past them, he turned his neck so that he could study their shiny brass fastenings. Down by his side, his fingers fluttered, rehearsing the lightning-quick action he would need. Up ahead, he saw that the corridor turned. *It might work. It just might…* Racing around the corner, he glanced back. He could hear his pursuers' stampeding boots, but they hadn't reached the corner, not yet. His arm flung toward a window, his fingers threw open the fastening at lightning speed, and…

He climbed out through the open window and shimmied along the sill. Harry reached the end and, grabbing a drainpipe, pushed the window shut behind him with his left boot. On one leg, he balanced at the sill's end, out of view. Although the sound was muffled by the glass, he heard his pursuers' boots thud past.

"Faster! He's only a boy!"

"Catch him!"

The Hotel Crosby Disappearing Act. As far as the hotel porters were concerned, he would have completely vanished, leaving no evidence at all. Who would be keen eyed enough to notice that the latch of a single window wasn't fastened? *But the trick's not done yet.* Balancing at the edge of a third-floor windowsill, he knew it was only a matter of time before someone looked up and spotted him. He needed to get down, and staring at the street below, he saw a way.

He waited, watching, calculating the right moment. Then he let go of the drainpipe, stepped off the sill, and plummeted thirty feet into a garbage cart trundling along the street.

Harry crashed deep into the garbage. Potato peelings, soggy newspaper, and the remains of meals slithered around him. Gagging, he gripped the edge of the cart and swung himself out onto the cobblestones, trying to ignore the slime leaking out of his shoes and the shouts of the driver as the cart trundled away.

He ignored the potato peelings on his jacket and the sludge dripping from his hair as he stumbled off down the alley, slanting left, weaving right until the Hotel Crosby was far behind. Stopping by a water pump, he worked the handle up and down, rinsing himself off. Then he hurried on through more alleys, more streets, until he arrived at the sidewalk corner where his friends were waiting, as had been agreed.

"Billie? Arthur? It's me!"

They didn't look up. They seemed deep in conversation. Billie was talking at high speed, waving her hands in the air, and Arthur was busily making notes on a little pad. *What are they doing?* Harry walked right up to Billie and tugged her sleeve.

"The plan worked great. Thanks, you two." Harry

knelt and picked up his shoeshine box, which Billie had kept safe for him. "Boris Zell, that's his full name, and he's staying in Room 760. And I found something else out too—it's serious."

Something was up with them. Billie had crossed her arms again, and Arthur was avoiding Harry's eye. But, at the same time, they couldn't help being interested in what he was saying, and the more the story flew out of him, the more interested they looked, particularly when he tugged the telegram from his pocket.

"So Herbie has been kidnapped?" Arthur pored over the telegram. "But that's terrible!"

"I'm trying to think of another explanation, Artie." Billie inspected the paper and handed it back to Harry. "But what Harry says adds up, unfortunately."

"We should tell the police." Arthur frowned. "Herbie could be in real danger—"

"It's not that easy!" Harry had already thought this through. "Who's going to believe us? Three kids, and all we've got is this telegram. They're not going to arrest Zell just because of that. The most they'll do is ask him a few questions, and then he'll know he's in danger. He'll check out of Hotel Crosby and vanish, simple as that. How are we going to help Herbie then?

No, we need to get into Zell's room and get more proof. Then the police will *have* to believe us."

He watched his friends. After a while, the two of them nodded, although Billie also wrinkled her nose.

"What's that smell?" Her eyes fixed on a potato peeling still on Harry's sleeve.

"I noticed it too." Trying to hide a smile, Arthur took a couple of steps back from Harry. "Pretty nasty."

"It doesn't matter." Harry brushed the peeling off. "I was just getting to that part when I had to make a run for it and—"

"You were seen?" Billie looked straight at him. "Right, we're definitely taking charge now!"

"What? Why?"

"You can't go back in there! Doesn't matter if you walk, sneak, or crawl, they'll be looking out for you."

"She's right, Harry." Arthur shrugged. "If they saw you, they'll know your face. You'll never get in, distraction or no distraction—"

"'Course I'm right!" Billie was pacing. "The Atlantic City Laundry Caper, Artie! That settles it."

The Atlantic City Laundry Caper. What was she talking about? *No time for Billie's stories*, thought Harry, spinning around. Apart from anything else, he was too busy thinking about something else Billie had said. She was right—it was going to be very hard to get back into the Hotel Crosby now that he had been seen—and that was extremely serious, as far as their plan was concerned. Harry ran across the street and hopped on top of a fire hydrant, nibbling a fingernail as he did so. *For Herbie's sake, he had to get back in—but how?* He peered up at the tall, dark shape of the hotel, a few streets away. Together with the buildings around it, it loomed high in the air...

High in the air.

"Harry?" Arthur's voice, strangely wobbly, called after him. "What are you doing?"

Harry stood on the fire hydrant, perfectly balanced. The plan to rescue Herbie was what mattered, and in the nick of time, he had thought up the next part of it. Not only that, but he knew where he would be able to get his hands on the equipment he needed. Not only *that*, but he had spotted, trundling toward him and gathering speed, a streetcar with the number 47 chalked on its front. He extended an arm.

"Harry!" It was Arthur again. "Why won't you listen to us? Why won't you..."

The streetcar swept past and Harry flew off the hydrant. Streetcar Number 47 would take him where he needed to go, and it wasn't hard to hold on, not after all the practice he had put into the trick of his, crossing Sixth Avenue by leaping between street-cars just like this one. *More than just a trick now*, he thought as he clung to the streetcar's side, ducking to avoid a shower of sparks. He swung around, trying to see his friends.

They were standing there, down the street. That troubled, puzzled look was back on Artie's face. Billie stood next to him, looking a little fiercer, but she had an arm around Artie for some reason. Harry stared and tried to make them out more clearly.

But sparks kept showering, making it impossible to see. And by the time the glittering flare had cleared, the streetcar had swerved around the corner.

His friends were nowhere to be seen.

Chapter 11

HARRY LEAPED OFF THE streetcar and landed on the sidewalk. The ride across Manhattan had blown most of the garbage smell out of his clothes, but he checked himself in a nearby grocer's window anyway and flicked a final potato peeling from behind his ear. Then he headed for the Wesley Jones Theater, his shoeshine box clutched under his arm.

Equipment. That was why he had come to this place, but it was also an opportunity to find out some useful information. After all, this was where Herbie's kidnapping had taken place. Swinging his shoeshine box off his shoulder, Harry set it up by the stage door and waited for the theater folk to drift in from the surrounding streets—Bruno the Strongman, the pearl-diving ladies, the Cossack dancers. Then he noticed someone standing next to him. It was Arnold, the gangly, wide-eyed stage manager with the weak left leg.

"Shoe shine, sir?" Harry peered up. "Just four cents, that's half price. It'd be an honor, sir, to shine the shoes of someone who works at the Wesley Jones Theater—it's my favorite theater in New York, sir."

A nice bit of patter. He could generally rely on getting himself a job, and the patter seemed to have done the trick on Arnold, although he didn't seem very happy about it. Sadly, the stage manager lifted his good leg and dumped the shoe on the end of it onto Harry's box.

"Yeah, I'll have a shoe shine." Arnold sighed. "Anything to make things look better on a day like today! D'you hear what happened here last night, shoeshine boy?"

"I did, sir." Harry rubbed in a blob of polish. "Poor Herbie Lemster…"

"Of course you've heard it! All of New York's talking about it!" Arnold rubbed at his eyes. "A mystery, that's what they're saying. But it's more than a mystery to us. It's a catastrophe! The most awful thing that's taken place at this theater! How could it happen? To one of our very own, shoeshine boy?"

What a state Arnold was in. The bruise he had suffered falling down the stairs was still on his forehead, dark and sore looking, but that was nothing compared to the sadness of his expression. His large eyes shone with tears, one of which splashed onto the shoe Harry was polishing, messing up the shine. Harry wiped it away and repolished the leather. Then he heard another voice, and looking around, he saw a face that was gloomier still.

"Terrible! Just terrible!"

It was Wesley Jones. The plump theater owner had just stumbled out of a horse-drawn cab. His pink hat was battered, his clothes were crumpled, and his plump body seemed to have crumpled too, his face sagging, dark bags under his eyes, and his skin drained to a sickly white. He glanced at Harry but hardly seemed to take him in as he kept talking to his stage manager.

"What can have become of him, Arnold? I haven't been able to sleep all night!"

"No one knows nothin', Mr. Jones." Arnold shook his head and pointed down at Harry. "You should treat yourself to a shoe shine too, Mr. Jones. This boy charges just four cents. Might cheer you up."

"Nothing could do that!" Wesley Jones tugged out a handkerchief and dabbed his eyes. "Still, only four cents, you say? To do my shoes?"

"Sure." Harry finished Arnold's toecaps with a flourish.

"Done. Come on up to my office and do my shoes, then." Wesley tossed Harry four cents, turned, and trod sadly into the theater. "All twenty pairs of them."

Twenty pairs? All for just four cents? Still, at least he had been invited into the theater. Harry's eyes flicked around as Wesley Jones led him through the gloomy backstage area, up a rickety staircase, and along various corridors. What a ramshackle building it was. In particular, the plumbing seemed completely chaotic, with countless pipes winding along the walls, taps and dials jutting off from them. Everywhere he looked, he could see pipes, many of them wobbling with the sheer pressure of the water inside, a few even sprouting leaks, but he reminded himself that he was hardly here to carry out a plumbing check.

Polish Wesley's shoes, perhaps do a bit more chatting, and slink off for the equipment. Harry followed Wesley all the way to his office, a surprisingly well-kept room with wallpaper that more or less clung to the wall, a plush rug, and a mantelpiece with various framed photographs on it. And, of course, there were Wesley's shoes, a whole rack of them in a cupboard. The plump theater owner collapsed into a chair by the desk, and Harry started work, unscrewing polish cans, fluttering cloths, and plunging into the conversation.

"So, hasn't anyone discovered *anything* about—"

"About poor Herbie? Nothing at all!" Wesley sank even further into his chair, his arms trailing over the sides. "The police were here late into the night. Detectives too. They worked the whole building over, bottom to top. But they ain't discovered a thing!" His face sagged, his eyes wet and mournful. "People say it's a trick gone wrong. They say it's dark forces. They say it's all kind of stuff. But what have they actually found out? Nothing!"

"Nothing, Mr. Jones?" Harry kept polishing.

"Not a darn thing!" One of Wesley's hands pounded the arm of his chair, while the other fluttered a handkerchief over his face, collecting the tears from his eyes. "All we've got is one thundering explosion, one storm of purple smoke, an intruder that no one actually saw, and some yelled-out words that no one understands. It's terrible, shoeshine boy. Just terrible!"

No information whatsoever. Harry tried to make out his reflection in the shoe he was polishing, which, for some reason, remained murky no matter how hard he rubbed. Perhaps he should tell Wesley what *he* knew? The distressed theater owner would almost certainly want to hear Harry's discovery about Herbie being kidnapped for his tricks—wouldn't he?

Possibly, thought Harry, polishing on. But, like the police, the theater owner was hardly going to take the word of a kid, particularly not a scruffy shoeshine boy reduced to cleaning twenty pairs of shoes for four cents. Like the police, at best Wesley would probably just make a few inquiries at the Hotel Crosby, and that would only alert Zell with disastrous results.

"What do you think, Arnold?" Wesley swung toward the office door, through which the stage manager had entered, his left leg dragging behind him. In his hands, he carried a tray with a teapot and cups on it, along with, curiously, a leather bag with a wrench protruding from it. "Who could be behind this horrible deed? Who'd want to harm Herbie? He hadn't an enemy in the world."

"Absolutely not, Mr. Jones! I never heard of no one not liking the guy, and I can't imagine it neither. He really was one gentle fella…"

The tea tray rattled in Arnold's wobbly grip, and he nearly dropped it, the leather bag also slithering out of his grasp. It was up to Harry, lightning quick, to leap across the rug and catch the teapot, the cups, and the saucers before they hit the rug. He just managed to grab the bag too, which he saw was full of all kinds of wrenches and other tools. Meanwhile, Wesley rose from his chair and lowered the unsteady Arnold into it in his place.

"Forgive my stage manager! He was so very fond of poor Herbie. Mind you, you're fond of all our fine company, aren't you, Arnold?" Wesley nodded at his stage manager's weakened leg. "He used to be a performer himself, a trapeze artist, until his unfortunate injury. So he knows how delicate performers can be, how carefully they must be looked after. You attend to their every need, do you not, Arnold?"

"That I do, Mr. Jones." Arnold lifted a feeble hand toward the bag of tools, which Harry gave him. "Was just about to do that plumbing job, sir."

"Ah yes, the plumbing." Wesley flung an arm at one of the theater's many wobbling pipes, which snaked across the office's ceiling. "We are attempting to install running water in every performer's dressing room. We prize our performers, so no effort shall be spared on their behalf. And none of them is prized more greatly than—"

"Than poor Herbie Lemster!" Arnold stared at the rug.

"Indeed!" Wesley tottered to the mantelpiece and the row of framed photographs which, Harry could now see, were of the theater's performers—Bruno the Strongman, the juggling acrobats, and the rest. "Why, I count him as one of my dearest friends. He has worked happily at this theater for no less than ten years."

A plump hand grabbed one of the framed photographs and held it aloft. Staring out of it, Herbie's face was wan and wrinkled. "He just did occasional appearances for me at first, but as our acquaintance grew, he did more and more until, in the end, he asked to become one of my regular acts, performing every night at the theater that I am proud to say he considers his true home."

"His home, nice and cozy." Arnold sadly contemplated a wrench.

"Yet it is his home no longer. Because he has disappeared. *Disappeared!*" Wesley held up the photograph, looked at Harry, and looked back at the picture again. "I don't suppose you polish picture frames, do you?"

Harry had just finished the shoes. He was about to protest that he had no silver polish, but Wesley had already fetched a small can out of a drawer and tossed it to him. For the next ten minutes, Harry polished the frame, the odd green polish making his skin itch. Herbie's face stared up at him, wrinkled, mysterious, and offering no help whatsoever. *But the mystery will be solved*, Harry decided, placing the photograph back on the mantelpiece.

He made his way down through the theater. Wesley and Arnold had left him alone to do the polishing task, and Harry knew it would be easy to slink off unnoticed, but he decided to visit the other performers. *Maybe they'll be more helpful.* Visiting their dressing rooms, he offered to shine their shoes and tried to ask a few questions. In the corner of each room, a sink gurgled mournfully, the result of Arnold's plumbing work, Harry deduced.

Not a scrap, not a snippet. The performers had no information for him. Still quivering with the shock of what had happened, they would be in an even worse state if they knew Herbie's possible fate, that he was probably being held captive by Boris Zell and forced to give up his tricks. *Good thing I'm on the case,* thought Harry as he slid out of the final dressing room and headed off toward his main task, the gathering of equipment.

Creeping down to the murky backstage area, he sought the place where he had sheltered the previous night after being swept in with the crowd. The wooden seaweed stood there, but he also made out several coils of rope hanging on the nearby wall, some with iron hooks on the end. *Perfect.* Harry chose the best rope, more than forty feet long, along with a medium-sized hook, and stuffed them under his jacket.

"Lost, shoeshine boy?"

It was Arnold. He was staring at Harry from a little way off in the backstage gloom. Harry wriggled, and the bulge in his jacket slid around the back. He walked toward the stage manager, his shoeshine box swinging from his hand.

"Took a wrong turn. Couldn't see where I was going." It was believable enough since the backstage area was very dark. "Sorry about that, Mr. Stage Manager."

Arnold said nothing. Wrapped up in mournful thoughts about Herbie, he also was clearly having more trouble with the theater's plumbing. His shirt-sleeves were soaked with water, and he had a wrench clutched in each hand. Silently, the limping figure led Harry to the stage door. Harry hurried out, but he must have accidentally knocked the stage manager off balance, because Arnold swayed and then steadied himself by gripping Harry's shoulder with a surprisingly fast, strong hand.

"Thanks for dropping by, shoeshine boy."

Another wobble. But Arnold steadied himself, and the hand let go. Harry offered a smile and hurried away from the theater.

The coil of rope and the hook were tucked neatly inside his jacket.

Chapter 12

HARRY STOPPED OFF AT the West Side docks, a favorite spot for practicing his tricks, quiet except for the lapping of the Hudson and the horns of passing ships. Among the warehouses and cranes, he spent nearly half an hour with the rope and hook, swinging them, spinning them, sending them flying. The trick was hard in all sorts of ways, and the way it needed to be set up was no exception.

Patiently, he perfected the throw, judging the flick of his wrist and jerking back his arm at exactly the right moment. By the time it worked, his arms and fingers ached from the practice. *Herbie's depending on it*, he thought, and the pain vanished as he ran off, weaving through the crowds, cabs, and horses at double speed, back toward the looming Hotel Crosby.

Billie and Arthur were right—there was no way on earth he could walk, sneak, or crawl back into that hotel. But walking, sneaking, or crawling wasn't what he had in mind. Tall though the drab hotel was, even taller buildings stood nearby, including the one across the street from it, an office building of some kind. A fire escape ran up that building's side, its rickety iron girders no more than twenty feet away from the hotel. Fixing his gaze on a spot about two-thirds of the way up the fire escape, Harry walked even faster, the coiled rope and hook dangling from his hand.

"Harry? Where have you been?"

Arthur was running toward him through the crowd. He had a slightly unusual look, his tie sticking out, his hair in a mess, his face flushed pink. *What's he been doing?* Looking around, Harry saw no sign of Billie and wondered what she was doing too. But then he spotted a clock over a nearby shop and knew there was no time for that. It had been nearly two hours since he had last been at the hotel, and Boris Zell could have been getting up to all manner of things. It was time to begin.

"I've been practicing, Artie!" He held up the rope. "Look!"

Odd. Usually, Arthur reacted to news of a new trick with interest, his eyes widening, sometimes his mouth falling wide open. But that wasn't happening now. Arthur just blinked at the rope, his face turning a little pinker, even red. *Maybe I just need to explain it a bit more*, Harry thought as he sprang toward the fire escape that ran up the side of the building near the hotel.

"Harry!" Arthur called after him. "Wait! I've got something to tell you… Me and Billie, we've…"

"Everyone at Hotel Crosby will be looking for me, Artie." Harry clanged up the iron stairs. "But that doesn't mean they'll be looking *up*—true?"

"Looking up? What do you mean?"

Harry sprinted upward, nearly ten stories, until he was level with the Hotel Crosby's roof. Pulling the rope off his shoulder, he twirled it, narrowed his eyes, and threw it. His arm ached from the practice, but it had definitely been worth it, because the hook at the rope's end soared neatly across the twenty-foot gap. It clanged against the railing that ran around the Hotel Crosby roof, looped around, and caught hold. Harry hauled at the rope until it was iron tight. *Artie'll understand the trick now.* From farther down the fire escape, he heard footsteps, and he turned to greet his even more red-faced friend, who was struggling up the last flight of steps toward him.

"The tightrope trick! Remember? Billie strung

the rope between two trees! I walked across it and wriggled my hands free of twenty-five knots at the same time."

"Harry…listen…" Arthur was out of breath. "Please, I…"

"If I can walk a tightrope while doing that, I can easily walk one with my hands free! I know it's higher up, but as long I stay on the rope, who cares how high it is?" Harry tore off his boots, tied the laces, and hung them around his neck. His bare feet flexed, ready for the walk. "So once I'm across, I just jump onto the roof and get into the hotel from there—"

"Harry!" Arthur had reached the fire escape landing and seen the taut rope. His face turned redder still, and he sputtered the words breathlessly out. "Why aren't you listening to me? We're a team, remember? Me, Billie, and—"

"I know we're a team! Just let me finish, Artie! So I go down into Room 760 and get in. I discover everything I can, then I run back up to the roof. I just need you to guard the rope, Artie—Artie?"

He had explained it all fairly clearly. Yes, he had been talking very fast, but surely the trick was plain to see. Particularly when he was actually balanced on the railing, one foot on the rope, the breeze from the street curling up around him. But Arthur still wasn't reacting in the usual way. He was just standing there, staring at the rope with that troubled look on his reddened face. Then he swung around, stomped over to the other side of the fire escape, and peered down. *Makes no sense at all*, thought Harry.

Unless...

"Where's Billie?"

"At last! Paying attention to me! There she is—down there!"

"What?"

"If you'd only listened, you'd already know. You see, you don't need to break into the hotel."

"Don't need to?" Harry looked down at the quivering rope. "But I'm almost there already—"

"So's Billie." Arthur shot an arm down at the street. "Look—right down there!"

Harry jumped down from the rope and leaped to the other side of the fire escape. And it was, he had to admit it, pretty astonishing.

Billie was walking up the hotel's front steps. But he wouldn't have recognized her if she hadn't been pointed out. An elegant silk gown swept down from her shoulders, peacock feathers sprouted from a bonnet, and most impressively, a large pair of wire-framed, dark-lensed spectacles wobbled on her nose, giving her a mysterious air. She was also several inches taller, and Harry glimpsed, just under the hem of the silk dress, some wooden blocks attached to the bottom of her boots. No wonder she was swaying slightly as she twirled a dainty umbrella and headed up toward those revolving hotel doors.

"Wha—What is she doing, Artie?"

"It's all based on the Atlantic City Laundry Caper."

"The what?" Vaguely, he remembered the words. "But—"

"It's a pretty simple business, really. I think you're going to like it, now that you're actually listening," said Arthur, swinging around. He put an arm around Harry, and a smile was back on his face. "So, back on the road, Billie rolled into Atlantic City, out of cash. She needed to get a job quick, so she tried to get one at a laundry, a fancy one for ladies and gents and their fancy clothes. The owner said she'd have to prove herself by washing a load of his stinky stockings and shirts, which she did and did it perfectly too.

"But the owner didn't give her the job and didn't pay her for washing the socks and shirts either! Just rolled around laughing, saying he'd never in a month of Sundays have a 'dirty hobo kid from New Orleans' messing up his fancy clean laundry! Big mistake. Billie grabbed a few bits and pieces off a laundry line and disguised herself as the servant of some rich lady who'd just arrived in town and—"

"But...how..." Harry tried to take it all in.

"I'm getting to that! She stuck blocks of wood under her shoes to make herself taller, pulled a bonnet over her face, and counted on the thick laundry steam to stop anyone from looking too closely. Clever, eh?" Arthur chuckled. "She just turned up at the door, asked the maids who worked there about placing a large order on behalf of her mistress for washing household linen. While they were fetching the owner, she slipped in, vanished into the steam, and tipped seventeen boxes of washing powder into one of the vats. Bubbles everywhere. That owner got himself a fancy clean laundry all right—took nearly two days to rinse the place out! Pretty good, don't you think?" Arthur pointed back down at the hotel steps. "And it's come in pretty handy for this Herbie business too, I'd say."

Billie was at the top of the steps now, bulked-up shoes, silk dress, and all. She was mumbling to the doorman, while making various grand gestures with the umbrella. And whatever she was saying, it seemed to work, because the doorman stood aside, and the elaborately disguised street girl swept through the revolving doors. The doors spun behind her, and Arthur nodded with a small, precise action.

"But this disguise—I don't see how it works." Harry stared at the still-spinning doors. "It's one thing to pretend to be a servant, but what's she pretending to be now?"

"That's mainly down to me." Another tweak of his tie. "I remembered reading that particular hotels are often popular with particular professions—word spreads, you see. So I said to myself, if this Boris Zell uses the Hotel Crosby, maybe other magicians do too. I ran back to the library and did some research, checked through old newspapers and hotel guides, and it turns out I was right. Magicians, illusionists, men of the theater—they've been using the Crosby for years.

"So would they be surprised if someone a bit exotic and theatrically dressed turned up—I don't think so." He was speaking quickly now. "The more exotic the better, probably. Billie and I had a quick think, and with the help of a few more books, we invented a whole new magician for her to be—Princess Moldo. That's who she's going to check in as!"

"Princess Moldo?" Harry had no idea what to say.

"The famous illusionist from Peru. I've been running around like mad ever since, finding out a few other things, buying the bits of costume, the dress, the umbrella—and not forgetting those dark spectacles." He pointed back down toward where Billie had been, wearing those glittering frames. "Do you know they actually come from Peru? From Lima? Found them in an antique shop—the Princess Moldo spectacles, I'm calling them."

"But costume, spectacles, umbrellas—it must have cost a fortune..." Harry butted in.

"A fair bit, yes, but my allowance covered it." Arthur tapped his wallet inside his jacket. "What else am I going to spend my money on, apart from my friends? Us and our plans, Harry, that's all that matters." Briefly, that troubled look returned. "To me, anyway..."

It might just work. Harry was still taking in a lot of what Arthur had said, but clearly this scheme was a good one, and so far it had worked. But would it continue to succeed? Getting through the door disguised as a Peruvian illusionist was clever. There was no question about that. But how exactly was Billie going to break into Room 760 itself? What about checking in at the hotel reception desk, which would need forms filled in and questions answered, during which time her disguise could easily be detected? All risky...

"Harry? What are you doing?"

"I'm going in too." Harry was back on the rail. "Like I said, I'm almost there anyway."

"But Billie and me... We're the ones who are doing this!"

"Why can't we carry out my plan too?" One foot edged out on the rope. "Doubles our chances in case something goes wrong. Herbie's been kidnapped, Artie! Zell could be doing all sorts of stuff to him, and he won't stop until he gets the secrets to Herbie's tricks and—"

"I know all that!" Arthur's face was red again, bright red. "Look, the whole Princess Moldo plan depends on the hotel staff not suspecting a thing! If you burst in there and get caught, then—"

"I'm not going to get caught, am I? Just guard the rope, Artie!"

"I don't need to! Just like you don't need to do this trick of yours!"

"I'll be back soon!"

"Harry! You're not listening to me again!"

"This is all for Herbie! That's what matters!"

"Of course it's about Herbie! Why else do you think me and Billie thought up our—"

"Remember the rope!"

"*Harry!* Stop acting like you don't want anything to do with me! I've got enough of that in my life already!"

Harry swung around and saw his friend's face. He had never seen it look quite like that before. It was trembling all over. Artie's hand was trembling too, as it reached into his pocket and tore out a letter, the letter to the school, the one Harry had helped snatch just a few hours ago.

"Next thing, you'll want to send me 452 miles away too! You won't have to listen to me then! Is that what you want? Is it? Is it—"

"Whoa!"

Harry had lost his balance. He recovered it the only way he could, by swinging his foot right around and planting it on the rope out over the street. He was balanced again, but he had also started the walk, and he couldn't stop. He had to keep walking, walking out over the street. *Perhaps that's for the best.* The echoes of Artie's words were still shuddering around him, making his face burn.

He had no idea how to reply. *Perhaps this way I don't have to—at least until I've thought of something to say*. His face still pulsing with heat, he angled his arms, steadied his legs, and bit his lip. *Need to concentrate on the rope walk*, he told himself—because it was turning out to be harder, much harder, than the one in the park.

The breeze sweeping up from the street was surprisingly powerful, full of the distant sounds of the street below. Harry glanced down, and his heart throbbed as he made out the tiny shapes of people, horses, cabs. The breeze flapped through his clothes, buffeting him about, and each time he lifted a foot from the rope he had to adjust his position, leaning into the gusts so that they wouldn't blow him off. *Completely different from the park.*

The wind was affecting the rope too, making it quiver, and it bounced slightly with every step. Harry's heart pounded and the palms of his hands, flung out on either side of him, were damp with sweat. He tried to think of nothing but his feet, edging along the rope step by step, and he kept leaning slightly into the wind, letting it support him…

With no warning, it changed direction.

Harry's arms flailed. Desperately, he tried to right himself as he tilted off the rope, unable to regain his balance. The wind spiraled around him with its noises of the far-below street, and Harry watched his arms blur through the air, felt his heart hammer inside his chest, and then, just in time, shot out a trembling leg.

The shift of weight tilted him back, just a little. He re-angled his arms, and that helped too. The wind buffeted, his clothes flapped, the rope shuddered. He was balanced again, but only just. His legs were weak and trembling, and his face clenched as tight as a fist. Concentrate. Think of nothing but the rope. And yet, even as Harry tried to do just that, he couldn't help noticing something out of the corner of his eye.

A window in a nearby building. It was level with him, ten stories up. Someone was watching him from it. A face. White hair, white eyebrows, a pair of staring eyes. A pale-suited figure, two hands resting neatly on the windowsill. Whoever he was, he was watching Harry, and something made Harry start turning his head to take in this figure properly, to see him more clearly.

The wind blew. Harry's arms sprang out on either side, but he was tilting off the rope again. His arms swirled, his heart pounded, his hands snatched at the empty air as he fought to pull himself back. Out of the corner of his eye, he saw that the pale-suited figure had vanished from the window.

Leaving nothing but dark, empty glass.

Chapter 13

HARRY HAD ONLY GLIMPSED his observer. But the observer himself had seen Harry plainly. Even now, as he stepped back up to the window, he continued to study the boy who, for some reason, was teetering on a rope stretched between two buildings, nearly ten stories up in the air.

About eleven years old. A street boy, from the look of him. A shoeshiner, given certain dark blotches on his clothes and face which the observer had spotted, even at this distance.

The man stood at the window. His suit was elegantly tailored, its cloth cream. Neatly manicured fingers rested on the polished windowsill, then rose to fetch a pen and a small leather notebook from their owner's pockets.

The boy had regained his balance. For the second time, he had nearly fallen, but his quick, nimble body had righted itself, and he was wobbling onward, making his way once more along the quivering rope. The man observed this and made a quick sketch of the two buildings and the rope. Next to it, the pen dotted out several lines of complicated numerical code, along with another symbol, a very curious one indeed.

At first, it was just a circle. But the steel nib shaded inside it, until it was black with ink. Further up the pen's length, a finger twitched, flicking a tiny button. A hiss, as white mist leaked out of the pen's nib. The mist thickened and drifted away.

Burned into the black circle, the white shape of a bird.

The boy had gone now. Only the rope remained. But the notes had been made. The man closed the leather book, revealing on its cover another white bird shape. He slid it back into his pocket with the pen.

One hand waved, dispersing any lingering traces of mist. Another lifted a telephone from the desk and dialed a number.

The telephone's earpiece buzzed. A voice in a language that wasn't English muttered through the crackles.

"It is possible," the man said, "that we have discovered a candidate."

Chapter 14

HARRY TOPPLED ONTO THE roof. He clung to a chimney stack, shaking all over. His body was weak, his heart still pounded, and when he lifted his hands from the chimney's brickwork, he saw they had left behind the shape of his palms and fingers in sweat. But he had made it back to the hotel, where he was sure the secret behind Herbie's disappearance would lie. Steadied by the thought, he set off across the roof, weaving past more chimney stacks toward the hatch he had spotted from the other side

Not even locked. Why would it be when there was no reason to think anyone could get onto a ten-story-high roof? But the door to Room 760 would be locked, that was for sure. Harry pulled the hatch open, slid down the ladder inside, and arrived at the top of a stairwell. Clattering down it, he peered around in his usual way for any stray bits of metal—a nail, a pin, anything at all useful.

Nothing in the stairwell, but as he reached the seventh floor and slid down a corridor, he saw a row of framed paintings on the wall. He stopped, lifted one down, and plucked the nail out of the plaster. *A pick.* Hurrying on, he prepared to inspect the lock on Zell's door and bend the nail into the right shape. But then he reached the corner, peered around it, and saw that he didn't need a lock pick after all.

The door to Room 760 was open. Next to it stood a cart of fresh linen, and two maids were hurrying into the room with fresh sheets. Harry tossed the nail away and ducked under a table by the wall. Watching from under the tablecloth, he waited until the maids' backs were turned. He glided through the door and rolled under the bed…

…straight into a peacock feather, an umbrella, and a pair of dark-lensed spectacles.

"Harry? I don't believe it! What are you doing here?"

"I came down from the roof…*Ow!*"

"Didn't Arthur find you? Didn't he tell you that we already had a plan?"

"Well, I…*mmmpf!*"

Billie was squashed under the bed. The springs above were close to her head, her silk dress and bonnet and umbrella were bulky, and her elbow had ended up in Harry's mouth, making it hard for him to speak. Another hand was right in front of his face, holding up a little slip of paper.

"Well, you better not interfere! This plan's working just dandy, and I'm not having you wreck it!" She pushed the bit of paper closer. "This is the seventh-floor linen-changing rotation. Artie got it by sweet-talking one of the maids who works here, so we knew I could just slip in here, nice and easy. 'Course, I had to get up here quick, but that was no trouble, 'cause it took no time at all to check in. Whenever they asked me questions, I just answered in Spanish, which is what they speak down Peru way, and Artie gave me a few phrases to remember."

The Princess Moldo spectacles, made in Lima itself, tilted on her nose. "So I get my key, I go up to my room, I walk straight on past it, and come up here instead. Pretty impressive, huh? So don't you try to interfere, you hear me?"

The elbow left Harry's mouth. But he wasn't sure what to say anyway. Point by point, Billie had removed any possible questions he might have had about Arthur's and her plan, which he could see really was a very good one.

"So how did you get in? You better not have been spotted!" Billie hissed.

"I…I came down from the roof," he said. "Threw a rope from the building next door. It was like the trick we did in the park, Billie…"

"You tightroped here?"

"Yes—ten stories up! It'll work for getting out too, I think, as long as Artie follows his instructions—"

"Artie? Instructions? So you *did* see him!"

Harry stopped talking as instantly as if the elbow had blocked his mouth again. But the Princess Moldo spectacles were even closer now. He was glad their lenses were so dark, because he sensed the eyes behind would be staring at him in a very unfriendly way indeed.

"You saw him! So he *would* have told you about our plan!"

"Yes but…"

"He told you, and you decided to come anyway. You ignored him!"

"I know…" Harry winced. "Except—"

"Typical! Can't you see how he's going to feel about that? With that father of his—*grrmpf!*"

The maids had hurried over to the bed, so Billie had been forced to swallow her words. But her face was still right in front of Harry's, those dark lenses glinting. He tried to wriggle away, but the bed wasn't wide enough, so the two of them were stuck there, unable to move, unable to speak, their noses less than an inch apart. For nearly a minute, they stayed like that, while the maids changed the sheets above and delicately dusted nearby ornaments. But at last, the maids left, shutting the door behind them, and Harry scrambled out.

"I'm sorry...I..."

"What's gotten into you, Harry?" Billie scrambled out too. "Running off all the time! Never listening to a word me and Artie say!"

"Herbie's been kidnapped! I can't just stand around—"

"Think me and Artie don't know that? We want to help Herbie too!"

"So let's rescue him!"

"That's what we are *doing*! That's what the Princess Moldo plan is all about, not that you've noticed. You know, Harry, when I met you and Artie, I thought you were the best friends I'd found since New Orleans." The glasses trembled and their lenses flashed. "Well, I was right about Artie—not so sure about you! All you care about is thinking up plans of your own like this tightroping business… Supposed to be impressed, am I?"

"It got me in here, didn't it?"

"But you don't *need* to be here! That's what I'm saying!"

"Of course I need to be here! Herbie's my friend."

"He's our friend too! We're meant to be doing this together. We're a team, aren't we? Oh, confound it!"

Harry ducked. Billie had hurled her silk umbrella straight at him, and he managed to dodge it, but only just. It smashed into the mantelpiece, splintering several of the ornaments the maids had so carefully dusted, and then flew off at an angle, thudding into a chair. Porcelain fragments fell from the mantelpiece, rocked on the floor, and went still.

"Billie?"

He swung around. Billie's arms were crossed, and those Princess Moldo glasses glared. But even worse, for the first time Harry could remember, Billie seemed to have nothing more to say. She just stood there, wobbling a bit on her heightened shoes, the peacock feathers on her bonnet sticking out at odd angles. Then she flopped down into the nearest chair.

"Confound it, I say!"

Harry turned and took in the hurled umbrella and the smashed porcelain. He thought about Arthur, back on the fire escape. *Enough of that in my life already…* Harry could hear those words as if they were echoing around him, and he winced again. "Listen, Billie. I'm sorry—"

He broke off when he saw the briefcase.

"Oh, no you don't, Harry! That's *mine*!"

It stood by a desk on the other side of the room. Boris Zell's briefcase, the same one that Harry had seen on the bulky magician's knee, the one with the telltale wisp of smoke. Harry was already gripping its handle. But Billie's hand was gripping it too, her Princess Moldo spectacles just an inch away from his nose again.

"I saw it first!" she sputtered.

"But—"

"Saw it the second I got in here!"

"Well, I saw it before that! Last night in the theater! Remember?"

Harry couldn't let go. If anything would reveal the truth about what had happened to Herbie, it would be the contents of that briefcase. *Later on, I'll sort things out with Billie, and with Arthur too*, he decided. For now, the briefcase was what mattered, and nothing else. He

133

tried to tug it free, and tugged harder and harder still, and then wondered, too late, if that was a good idea.

"Watch out!"

He stumbled back. The briefcase had split open. A monkey skull, two candlesticks, and a heavy book tumbled onto the floor. But he wasn't worried about those. He watched as a corked jar of purple powder spun out of the briefcase, slammed onto the floor, and cracked. A flash of light, the room thundered, and he was thrown straight into a wall.

Purple smoke everywhere. Harry tasted the chemicals in his mouth again. He heard the sound of tinkling glass and knew the window had blown out. At least he had ended up in a more comfortable position this time, sliding down onto the hotel room's rug rather than crashing into the sidewalk. Struggling up, he groped through the fumes, among which he made out Billie's face, along with a finger pointing at him.

"Now look what you've gone and done!"

"You should have just let me open it carefully!"

"Why? I'm the one who's investigating this hotel room! Me—Princess Moldo, I mean."

"Well, at least I was right about Zell." Harry knelt over the shattered remains of the jar. "He's behind the explosion in Herbie's dressing room. We know that for sure now."

"Don't know too much else though." Billie peered through the plumes of smoke. "So Boris explodes something in the dressing room—but how'd he get in there? How'd he get out again, dragging Herbie? No one saw nobody go in or out, remember?"

It was true. Harry sniffed the smoke. That was all it was—smoke. Billie was right. It told him nothing. Zell had kidnapped Herbie, and Harry knew the magician's motive, thanks to the telegram from Chicago. But how had he done it? That was the true mystery, and the smoke, still drifting around him, revealed nothing about it.

The plumes swirled. And the smoke *did* reveal something. Harry flinched, and the smoke he had sniffed flew out of his nostrils in two little clouds. Across the room, Billie was looking alarmed too.

There right in front of them, materializing out of the smoke, was Boris Zell.

Chapter 15

"YOU! BOY FROM THEATER!"

The huge magician's eyes glittered in the smoke. His accented voice boomed through the drifting plumes, making them thrash and swirl. Harry wondered if he really did have some sort of magical power. How else had he managed to appear so silently, as if summoned by the smoke? How had he managed to track Harry and his friends down at the library? But there really wasn't time to worry about any that, because Zell, magical or not, was lunging through the smog, a burly hand outstretched, and it was time to run for it, as fast as Harry possibly could.

"Quick, Billie!"

No need to tell her. She was already running. Together they dodged through the smoke, ducked past the lunging arm, and tried to get through the doorway, tangling up in Billie's billowing silk dress and peacock-feathered bonnet. A knot of arms, legs, feathers, and genuine Peruvian spectacles, they thudded out onto the corridor floor.

"Out of my way, Harry!"

"I'm tangled up!"

"Bad enough you not letting no one else break into this place! Now you're not letting no one but you escape from it neither!"

"Just run!"

"Don't you tell me what to do!"

"Run!"

"I'm not taking orders from you no more!"

"Run!"

Zell's arm swooped into the corridor. Billie scrambled along the hall, hopped onto the banister of a nearby staircase, and slid down it. She crossed her arms, and those Princess Moldo spectacles remained fixed on Harry, glaring with rage as she gathered speed.

"Boy! You come here!"

No time to think. Zell was nearly upon him. The burly magician had lurched through the doorway, and Harry took off in the opposite direction from Billie, racing up the corridor. He could hear heavy gasps behind him, could feel the tips of those huge fingers touching the back of his jacket, but his legs sprang to life and he flew down the corridor. He slammed into the stairwell and scrambled upward. Spiraling up the steps, he heard a door slam below and knew Boris was in the stairwell too, but he flew up the last flight of stairs to the ladder, burst through the hatch, and ran between the chimney stacks.

He saw the roof's edge and the tightrope stretching away, and his heart throbbed again at the thought of the walk that lay ahead—but he knew he had no choice. With a leap, he was up on the railing, a foot on the rope. He was ready. A single step would send him off on the journey across the street. He swung around for one last look at his terrifying foe.

Zell didn't seem quite so terrifying now. Across the roof, he was stumbling toward Harry but slowly. Sweat poured off his face, winding into his mustache and making it droop. His burly arms drooped too, sapped of strength. Tottering, he gripped a chimney stack to keep himself upright.

"You were there that night!" He pointed feebly at Harry. "The Wesley Jones Theater… Maybe you saw something… Help me…"

"Why would I help you?" The words just flew out. "You—you're behind it all! The smoke, the explosion, everything! You're the one who kidnapped Herbie."

A mistake. Harry's lips clenched tight. But it was too late. The words were already trembling through the air, and now Zell would know how much had already been discovered. *Better get on with the escape.* He turned back and took his first step along the rope but then froze as he heard Zell's next words.

"Kidnap Herbie? Why would I do that? Why would I do anything of the sort to a man who is my oldest, dearest friend?"

Harry toppled. His feet fumbled and slipped.

And he fell straight off the rope.

Chapter 16

Harry's hand caught the rope as he dropped. He jerked to a halt and hung there, dangling. But his grip was already weakening. He stared down and saw his feet swaying over the far-below street. He stared up and saw his fingers steadily losing their hold, the strength draining from them one by one...

He flew up through the air. A burly hand had circled his wrist, and he was being hoisted up onto the roof. He collapsed in a heap and looked up to see Boris Zell releasing his wrist and sinking onto the roof too, looking more exhausted than ever. Harry tried to scrabble away.

"You're lying! Herbie's my friend! Not yours!"

"Believe what you like..." The heavily accented voice was a feeble gasp. "What do I care? You were my only clue, boy... But I was mistaken. I see that now..."

"Me? *Your*...clue?" Harry kept scrabbling, but his back was against the rail at the edge of the roof.

"The boy must have something to do with it, I think... Herbie disappears, and the next day I see a boy who was at the theater when I visit a library... Strange, I think..."

"Not really! We had every reason to go to the library. We needed to find out information about you, didn't we? How come *you* were there—that's the strange thing!"

"I went to look up books about disappearing acts." Zell shrugged. "I cannot understand how Herbie was snatched away... I think maybe a book will tell me..."

Not a bad answer, thought Harry. The library would be full of such books. It might have been clever to have looked at a few himself.

His eyes kept darting around, searching for a way to escape. There were plenty of other things that needed explaining, and they would need answers every bit as good.

"Who cares about the library? What about the jar of purple smoke powder in your briefcase? The same purple smoke that went off that night in Herbie's dressing room." Harry jabbed an accusing finger. "Explain that, Boris Zell!"

Zell said nothing. He just crouched there, still recovering his breath. His mustache drooped even more forlornly. He wasn't to be trusted. Harry was sure of it.

"Purple smoke?" Boris sighed. "The Magician's Fire, you mean. Very well, I shall explain it. It is a simple enough device. A powder that, when thrown to the ground, explodes into smoke—useful for magicians who wish to hide something from their audience. Other powders do this, but the Magician's Fire is a variety I mix myself to achieve the attractive purple color of the smoke." He struggled up. "It is not so dangerous, boy."

True enough, thought Harry. He himself had just been caught in an explosion of it, and it hadn't done any harm. It had just thrown him against a wall, smashed out a window, and clouded things up a bit. Clouded things up like Zell was doing now, perhaps? Remembering something, Harry pulled from his pocket the telegram from Oscar P. Munz, owner of the Chicago theater.

"So, maybe the smoke isn't dangerous. But it still belongs to you. And it blew up in Herbie's room when he disappeared! How come something only you own ends up there that night?" He waved the telegram.

143

"And listen, I may not know how you kidnapped Herbie, but I know why. This tells me, plain as day."

"Does it?" Boris stared at the telegram. Those cruel eyes, Harry noticed, bulged with a watery sheen.

"It's from the next theater you're playing, in Chicago. It says you have agreed to perform Herbie's tricks there. Bicycling over Spikes! The Flying Knives! Spider up Sleeve! You kidnapped him to get the secret of those tricks. You've got him hidden somewhere, your prisoner, until he tells you what you want to know."

"We will talk about this one thing at a time, yes?" Zell stared intently at Harry. "First, purple smoke. Why was it in Herbie's dressing room? The answer is simple, boy. I had given it to him just an hour before. A whole jar of Magician's Fire. A gift from me, Boris Zell, to my dear old friend."

"Gave it to him?"

"Twenty years I have known Herbie Lemster!" Zell said. "We meet backstage in a Prague theater when I was a penniless young magician. For a few weeks we travel together, him teaching me all he knew. 'Dear Mr. Herbie,' that is what I call him then, and that is what I call him ever after, whenever we meet again over the years that come, as we travel the roads of Europe. In theaters, in city squares, on platforms waiting for trains—we see each other and 'Dear Mr. Herbie,' I always say to him, and he always shakes my hand, he always smiles! To be traveling magician, it is not always easy, boy, and what greater comfort than a friend!" Boris hunched weakly. "But our meetings were not to last.

"About three years ago, I notice it—I had not seen Mr. Herbie for a while. Another month goes by, then another, then a year—I ask myself, where is he? Is he ill? Does he perform magic no longer? I have no address for him, nor he for me. We are magicians of the road, with no home to our name. I tell myself, I have lost my friend forever!"

Boris wiped the tears from his mustache. "But my life goes on. My travels continue. In hope of finding Herbie, I journey further. To Moscow, St. Petersburg in the north. To Constantinople in the south. More years go by. Like many magicians, I buy ticket for America, to continue my travels there. I come to this city of New York, arriving just three days ago…"

Interesting story, thought Harry. Believable too— not least because of the speed at which it had flown from Boris's mouth, no hesitation or stuttering at all. Besides, a piece of information had caught his attention, a piece of information that, if true, might make this whole business very different indeed. Harry leaned closer and listened with care.

"I check into this hotel," Boris continued. "I try to think how to set up business in this new country. I make telephone calls, I send telegram—yes, I will explain that, I promise." He pointed at the telegram in Harry's hand. "I make plans to tour Pittsburgh, to Buffalo, to Toronto, to Chicago. All day work, very hard. But then, at four o'clock yesterday afternoon…" For the first time, a smile appeared on Boris's face.

"I pick up a newspaper in the hotel lobby. Just by chance, you understand. I open it, and there is an advertisement for some Wesley Jones Theater. It lists acts—a strongman, dancers, so on. And there at the bottom, I see his name! Herbie Lemster, magician. Dear Mr. Herbie, who I lose for so long, is here! I read his name! I throw newspaper in air! I go and find him. I look him up."

"When exactly was that?" Harry walked over to Boris.

"Yesterday! Six o'clock. Just before evening show. I went to the stage door and asked for him, but they told me that he was busy. But no matter, I go ahead with my plan anyway."

"Your plan?"

"My plan to work with Herbie Lemster. No more meetings on road. We shall travel that road together! I write this to him in a note and leave it for him. I shake when I write, I am so excited! I say we meet after show. I leave a jar of Magician's Fire too—a gift for dear Mr. Herbie. Then I go watch. I shake when I see Herbie again—I remember what good magician he is. But more, what a good friend he is. He and I, we will make success together, I know it! Show ends and I go to wait at stage door but then—*BOOM*! Magician's Fire explode! Herbie disappear!"

It makes sense. Every bit of Boris's story fit neatly with what Harry knew. He spotted the snake on the burly man's cape, catching the sunlight. *A brooch, that's all—for the Order of Gabrovo. Most magicians in Europe probably belong to a society of some kind.* Looking down, Harry noticed that the telegram was still in his hands, and he studied it thoughtfully.

"So the telegram from Chicago…"

"Ah yes." Boris took the telegram from Harry. "You think it strange that I say I can perform these tricks. You think, because they are Herbie's, that I must steal them to make them my own? But why would I need to do such a thing? Herbie train me, remember? He teach me these tricks, one by one! He make me watch him, night after night, and bit by bit I spot things, work things out. It is the 'great game of magic,' Herbie says. These tricks, I have performed them all my life! Why wouldn't I write about them in telegram to Chicago?"

Harry scrunched the telegram into a ball and tossed it away. Everything he had thought about this business had turned out not to be the case, and he felt his face warm with a blush. But he stood up and walked around, letting the rooftop breeze cool him. No point in worrying about any of that. Apart from anything else, he had already spotted a whole new way of investigating the affair. His thoughts turned again to that little bit of information Boris had revealed just a few minutes ago.

"Mr. Zell, you say you lost touch with Herbie about three years ago?"

"Why yes! Three years ago, yes!"

"Before that, for nearly twenty years, you saw him every few months?"

"Yes! In theaters. In city squares. In—"

"And during all that time, you and Herbie—you were in Europe?"

"Yes! I already say this!"

"Not America, then?"

"No! Berlin, Paris, Prague...only Europe! Why you ask this? And why you walk like that?"

Harry was pacing circles around Boris. He regarded him from every angle, and he considered what the magician had said from every angle. It was the clue he needed, the telltale bulge, the tiny twitch that would give the whole trick away. He thought it through. According to Boris, Herbie Lemster had been working as a magician in Europe until just three years ago. Harry saw no reason to disbelieve him. It fit with everything else he said. But it didn't fit with something someone else had said, and that someone was...

Wesley Jones.

Wesley Jones, owner of the Wesley Jones Theater. The plump gentleman had said that Herbie had been working happily for his theater here in New York for the last *ten* years. *"Why, I count him as one of dearest friends!"* Harry thought back to that conversation in the theater owner's office. He remembered it quite clearly. He was sure of that.

"Boy? You make me dizzy!"

Harry was pacing even faster. Boris had become a blur, but he wasn't thinking about the magician anymore. He was thinking about every word he had heard as he crouched polishing those twenty pairs of shoes. How distressed the theater owner had seemed. How bewildered by what had taken place.

How forcefully he had said, several times, that he and his stage manager cared deeply for the performers at their theater, how they were even installing a new plumbing system for their comfort. And, most importantly, how one performer, Herbie Lemster, had been so happy at the theater that he had worked there for *ten* years—which now turned out to be untrue.

Wesley had lied. But why? What did it mean? Harry had no idea, but he could feel a strange coldness spreading through him. He pulled his jacket close, but the feeling kept spreading. The more he thought about Herbie and that conversation with Wesley Jones...

"It's him! Look!"

"The boy! The one who threw himself out the window!"

"Get him!"

The hotel porters. Far across the roof, they were clambering out of the hatch, two of them. Wisps of purple smoke rose from their clothes. Clearly, they had been alerted by the explosion in Room 760. Boris could explain everything, but how long would that take? *I've lost enough time already.*

"Boy! What you doing? You crazy?" shouted Zell.

Harry felt bad about Boris. He had just started getting to know him, and far from being menacing, the burly magician seemed rather friendly. But there really was no time—the porters were already stumbling between the chimney stacks, and he needed to be quick. With a leap, he was at the railing again, balanced on the rope. His boots dangled around his neck, his arms wavered at his sides, and he was high over the street, one foot following the other, even faster than before...

"Come back, boy!" Zell's cry echoed after him. "I already had to rescue you! Stop! Stop—"

"I'll be careful! It's for Herbie's sake, Mr. Zell!"

Harry's feet flashed along the rope. The wind blew; the rope shuddered; the horses and people and cabs looked just as tiny down on the street below. But for some reason his legs didn't feel as weak this time. His heart wasn't pounding as fast, and his feet were picking up speed. He wondered if it was because he had done the tightrope walk one time before, had even survived a fall from it, thanks to Boris Zell. Perhaps that was why he felt more confident now, surer in his step. But he knew there was another reason too, a reason that burned deep inside him, powering him on...

Get to the theater.

A gust of wind buffeted him, but he was ready. When it swung around behind him, he even used it, letting it push him along. His fists were clenched, his feet kept flashing along, and he was already halfway. The rope bounced with every step, but Harry decided to use that too, letting the energy in the rope spring him along, powering him faster. Why, he wasn't just tightrope-walking; he was tightrope-*running*—and a good thing too. *Get to the theater.* Only a few steps left, and he took them even faster, leaping, springing along the rope, and landing with a neat chime on the iron fire escape…

…where he was knocked straight off his feet by Arthur, racing down the stairs.

Chapter 17

HARRY! WHAT WERE YOU doing on the roof—*Ow!*" Arthur tumbled down the fire escape. "I was watching you."

"You were?" Tangled up with his friend, Harry tumbled too.

"Yes! I saw you. With Boris Zell! *Ouch!*"

"I was talking to him—"

"I know you were talking! But what about? I couldn't hear—*Look out!*"

They were gathering speed. Harry watched Arthur's face speed past and snatched at the railings, but he was traveling too fast. He tumbled onward and made out a familiar voice and some footsteps clanging up the steps.

"So I got out easy, Harry. No fancy tightrope-walking needed by me! The Princess Moldo trick, that's all. I just walked out through the lobby, cool as a cucumber, nobody asking me a single question. Not that you care about that—*Ooof!*"

They slammed right into her. Billie must have seen them coming, but their speed had clearly taken her by surprise, and she was part of their tangle now, tumbling downward. The silk dress ripped, the bonnet crumpled, the peacock feathers flew through the air, and Harry's flailing arm tore the Princess Moldo glasses right off Billie's face. They had snagged on his jacket's sleeve. He tried to pull them off, hoping to give them back to her, but they were too firmly lodged, one of the wire arms twisted through the lining.

"Don't look so surprised, Harry. You've wrecked the plan—why not wreck the costume as well?"

"I didn't mean to wreck... I was just trying to... *Ow!*"

They had toppled down onto one of the fire escape landings, Harry slamming his head hard against its rails. He sprawled there and wondered if he was still falling, because his head was spinning so fast. He stumbled up and immediately fell down again. His head throbbed and his vision blurred, but he just about managed to make out his friends, still tangled up with him.

"You should have left it to me and Artie!" Billie

sat up first, grabbing her bonnet from under Arthur's foot and jamming it on her head again. "If you hadn't blundered in and set off that explosion of smoke, I'd probably still be up there. Spying on Boris from under the bed. I'd have found out all kinds of things. Instead we've all of us found out nothing. Diddly-squat!"

"You're wrong about that, Billie. Harry may have found out quite a bit!" Arthur tugged at a peacock feather in his hair. "He's been up on the hotel roof for nearly ten minutes talking with Zell. I saw them."

"Really?" Billie sputtered.

"Not that he's told me much about it, mind." Arthur frowned. "Have you, Harry?"

"I'm sorry…" Harry gasped, still struggling to get up. "I—"

"So tell us now, Harry." Billie grabbed Harry's sleeve. "It's the least you owe us after what you've done—especially to Artie!"

"It's true." Arthur hesitated and folded his arms. "I'm sorry I got angry before, Harry—but I meant what I said. My whole life, I've been treated like I'm nothing important. Meeting you and Billie—well, it's the first time I've felt I'm actually somebody…"

"True of all of us!" Billie gripped Harry's sleeve tighter. "What would I be without the two of you to help? A scruffy New Orleans street girl, doing crummy jobs and struggling to get by, that's all. As for you, Harry, where would you be if me and Artie hadn't noticed your tricks? So tell us! *Tell us what happened!*"

"I'll try… It's not easy… I don't understand most of it myself yet…" At last, Harry managed to stumble up. He tried to make out his friends more clearly, but his vision was too blurred. And he tried to take in everything they had said, but his head was still spinning. "I'm sorry, Artie. Of course I think you're important… I…" *Get to the theater*. His head spun even faster as he stumbled down the fire escape toward the street below. "I'll try to explain… Boris Zell… He's different from what I thought…"

"Different how?" Billie clanged after him, and Arthur wasn't far behind.

"Well, he's Herbie's friend…" Waves of dizziness swept over him.

"Friend? Why did he kidnap him, then?"

"He didn't…" *Get to the theater*.

"Who did, then?"

"I don't know… Not yet…"

"What exactly did Boris say? You've got to tell us, Harry!"

Harry's head spun faster. His stomach throbbed,

deep inside, and he thought he was going to throw up. The iron struts of the fire escape were a blurred jumble. The words in his head were a jumble too. He had to get away from his friends' questions, however much he wanted to answer them, because each one was only making him dizzier.

Even if he managed to stutter something out, that would only lead them to ask more questions, needing more answers, taking longer and longer...and how would that help Herbie? *Get to the theater*, he thought. *That's the only thing that matters*. He stumbled down onto the fire escape's next landing.

"I'll tell you as soon as I can... It's too complicated... There isn't time... Herbie, he's in trouble... I've got to go... I..."

He saw the Number 47 streetcar rattling along the street toward him three stories below.

"Harry!"

"Come back!"

He was throwing himself off the fire escape. With a life of its own, his fist was gripping the iron rail. His arm straightened, his body swung, and he was tumbling toward the rattling streetcar's roof twenty feet below. He thudded onto the roof, just inches away from the deadly overhead cables, and sprawled there as the streetcar rattled away, sparks showering around him. Still dizzy, he sat up and looked back.

"I'm sorry…"

The words were snatched by the wind. His friends back on the fire escape clearly hadn't heard them at all. Billie pounded about on the landing; Arthur tore the peacock feather out of his hair and threw it to the ground. All around them lay the wreckage of their carefully put together costume—the squashed bonnet, the torn dress.

Remembering the Princess Moldo spectacles, genuinely made in Lima itself, Harry fumbled with his jacket and managed to untangle them at last. Both lenses were smashed, and the wire frames were bent out of shape. He tried to bend them back, but fragments of glass just fell out of the frames.

How can it have ended up like this? he thought as he looked back up at the two shapes on the fire escape, his friends. But they were too far away to make out properly now. He slid the broken glasses into his pocket. He would give them back to them later. *Perhaps that'll make things better*, he told himself.

Although, as he rattled off across Manhattan to the Wesley Jones Theater, he thought it probably wouldn't.

Chapter 18

THE STREETCAR CLATTERED PAST the Wesley Jones Theater, and Harry jumped off. He touched his head and felt a swelling bruise, but the dizziness was nearly gone. It kept fading as he slid into the laughing, chattering crowd that was pouring out from the theater's afternoon show. No shoeshine plan was necessary to get backstage this time—just a simple break-in. He weaved through the crowd until he was in the foyer and glanced about, searching for a way. Seeing a door, he ducked across, checked that no one was looking, and pushed the handle up. Not even locked. He slid through and closed the door behind him.

He was in a dimly lit corridor. He climbed a rickety staircase. More corridors, more staircases flashed by, and pipes, hundreds of them, throbbed and wobbled around him. Harry stared at them because almost everything Wesley had said seemed suspicious now, and the stuff about the plumbing improvements was no exception. Finding another staircase, he recognized it as the one he had climbed with Wesley Jones that morning and swiftly scrambled to the door at the top, placed an ear against it, and, checking no one was inside, crept in.

"He has worked happily at this theater for no less than ten years…"

Harry stood in the middle of Wesley Jones's office. He saw the plush rug and the cupboard containing the twenty pairs of shoes. The theater owner's words echoed back to him—words which Harry now knew were not entirely true. Why had Wesley lied? Why had he exaggerated the length of time Herbie had worked here? Could it be that he wished to make the old magician's happiness with his job at the theater as convincing as possible? If so, why?

The coldness Harry had felt on the roof crept into him again, and he started pacing the room, partly to keep warm, partly to help himself think. Five times, he circled the office, and then he dropped into Wesley Jones's leather chair, positioning himself just as the theater owner had earlier that day, sliding

into the curved hollow left by that plump figure—
unpleasant but worth it, if it helped him see things
from Wesley's point of view.

The mantelpiece. There in front in Harry, as he sat
in Wesley's chair, was that carved marble bulk, with
its framed photographs of the performers running
along the top. All through his weeping, Wesley had
been staring right at those photographs, but why?
Harry was out of the chair, inspecting the mantelpiece and lifting each frame. His brain still couldn't
piece together this business, but for the moment
his fingers were doing the thinking. They scurried
about, checking the frames and exploring the edge
of the mantelpiece. From its frame, Herbie's face
peered out, as mysterious and wrinkled as ever...

Harry's fingers brushed against something.

On the underside of the mantelpiece, just
beneath Herbie's photograph, was a bump, a metal
tip. Harry's fingers explored and managed to grip
its edge. He pulled, and an inch-long stub of metal
slid out, a hinge at its base. *Some sort of switch.* He
flicked it and toppled back as the whole mantelpiece
swung out from the wall, its heavy marble bulk
moving smoothly and silently, supported on huge
iron hinges that glistened with oil. Harry sprawled

on the plush rug, staring at the dark doorway that had been revealed, before scrambling up and springing into the gloom.

A spiral staircase. Harry clattered down it, his hand clutching the rail. Light from Wesley's office spilled down from above, revealing crumbling walls, rotten timbers, and yet more throbbing pipes. Harry heard the roar of the water inside them and wondered again about the plumbing work Wesley had mentioned and whether it was really just to improve the running water in the dressing rooms.

He plunged deeper into the gloom. The only light came from an iron lamp, dangling from a chain, with a candle flickering inside. The stairs led to a windowless room that seemed to be full of water: black, rippling, the candlelight glimmering on its surface. Harry bent down and dipped his hand in the water. Icy cold. Harry flinched and flinched again as, right in the middle of the water-filled gloom, he made out a cage.

It was large, rectangular, and made of iron. Across the front of it, Harry noticed some letters. Candlelight flickered weakly off them, but he couldn't quite make them out.

He stared at a figure inside the cage, knee-deep

in water. Knotted ropes crisscrossed his body and a gag distorted his face, but Harry recognized him immediately.

It was Herbie.

Chapter 19

BICYCLING OVER SPIKES. THE FLYING KNIVES, Spider up Sleeve. Harry remembered all his old friend's tricks and how they had fascinated him. But none of them had ever made him feel as astonished and horrified as he felt now, seeing Herbie in the cage. Harry stood at the bottom of the stairs, the black water lapping at his boots, for some time before he realized that the old man was jiggling in his chair, staring at him with bulging eyes, and trying to say something.

"Mmmmmmph!"

Harry splashed into the water. It reached halfway up his legs, but he waded to the cage and gripped its bars. Herbie's mouth was struggling to shape words around the cloth gag, and Harry wondered if he could somehow read those struggling lips. He tried to do that, only to realize that the frail magician was jerking his head back toward the dangling iron lamp. Harry splashed over and found, just next to the candle, a key. Twisting it in the lock, he slid the door across and waded into the cage. He tried to undo the old man's gag, but the knot securing it was tight. He tugged at it, pried it, and finally pulled it loose, only to collapse back into the water with a splash, knocked off balance by the force of the old man's cry.

"Harry! What are you doing here? You are in danger! Don't you realize?"

Harry sprawled in the water. Soaked, he struggled back up. Herbie's cry still echoed, but the power of it seemed to have exhausted the old man, and he was slumped in his chair. Harry's fingers probed the ropes that held the old man, their knots even tighter than the gag's. He worked them and tried to answer Herbie's questions.

"I'm here to rescue you, Herbie. I watched the window of your dressing room—saw what happened before you disappeared. I thought Boris Zell was behind it but…"

"Boris?" The old man's face lifted, his eyes shimmering. All that was left of his voice was a feeble gasp. "Why would Boris do such a thing? He is my oldest friend—"

"I know that now." Harry kept working at the knots. "You trained him. You met each other all over Europe. You saw each other at theaters, in city squares—"

"If only I had stayed in Europe," wailed Herbie. "If only I had never come to New York…if only I had never set eyes on the Cruel Theater of Wesley Jones!"

Tears traveled down the complicated pathways of the old man's wrinkled face. His lips trembled and went still, a sorry sight. Harry hoped that Herbie would gather enough strength to continue with his tale soon. Clever though it had been to discover the mantelpiece trick, he still had no idea what was going on, and so far his elderly friend's gasps had just confused things further.

"The Cruel Theater of Wesley Jones? What do you mean?"

"I signed Wesley's contract in desperate times…" The gasps could only just be heard. "I had fallen ill on the journey across the Atlantic, and for nearly a month after arriving in this hard city, I could not work—I was penniless! So when I met Wesley, I signed. I agreed to perform at his grubby theater for a grubby wage, show after show, night after night. But no one gets out of Wesley's contracts. I know that now…"

"How come?"

"Because Wesley Jones never lets go of a talented performer! Once he has you in his grip, he never relents. All of us at this theater are forced to perform endlessly for a pittance, but no one dares leave. Some he has tricked into debt, and if they dare defy him, he will have not only them but anyone they hold dear thrown out on the street, penniless. Others he controls thanks to harboring little secrets from their past, petty crimes or shameful doings, proof of which he keeps filed away in a hidden safe. Again, if they defy him, he will destroy them utterly. What power he has!"

The old man clutched his throat, every word causing him pain. "And then there are those, such as myself, whom he controls by sheer menace alone. Desperate, we wish to leave this dreadful place. And yet we dare not, for fear of what would happen if we tried. A terrible threat hangs over us…"

"What?" Harry was trying to take it all in.

"What? Who, you mean. Why, Arnold, of course! Stage manager…and notorious failed trapeze artist."

Harry's fingers tore at the knots. Each one was more intricate than the last, but he was prying them loose, and the terrible business of Herbie's disappearance also was unraveling. Harry remembered his conversations with the theater's performers and how mournful they had been about Herbie. Perhaps they were sad for other reasons too. As for Arnold, the gangly stage manager with his weakened leg seemed an unlikely threat, but Harry also remembered that moment when Arnold had shown him out of the theater and had gripped his shoulder with surprising strength.

"Failed trapeze artist? But Wesley Jones said he was a successful one who injured himself years ago."

"He injured himself trying to outdo all other performers." Herbie glanced fearfully around the gloom. "Fell from the trapeze and damaged his left leg beyond repair—but that doesn't mean the rest of him isn't strong and fit. Every one of Arnold's limbs, apart from that left leg, harbors a trapeze artist's strength—a strength gone wild from frustration at his thwarted performer's ambition." The voice kept going, a tangle of whimpers and sobs.

"Unable to thrill audiences any longer, he nurses a profound hatred of anyone who can. If any of us dares step out of line, Wesley sends Arnold to their dressing room, and they quickly regret it. As for any of us who dares to go near another theater to discuss possible work—why, Arnold finds out and the regrets are more pitiful still! The sorry offender is dragged down to this terrible place…with its terrible words…"

"Words? What do you mean?"

"Why, the motto Wesley snarls at us, his enslaved performers, every day."

A terrified finger pointed up. Harry looked up at the iron letters on the cage. They gleamed in the candlelight, and now he could make them out quite clearly. *What's yours is mine and always shall be.* Harry stared and remembered hearing those words trembling through Herbie's dressing room window as the mysterious intruder grappled with the spindly old man. His fingers tore at the intricate knots with even greater speed.

"Wesley's control is total. Like a gangster, his menaces hold us in line. I tried to shield you from it, Harry. Why else do you think I never let you backstage? Or met you after a show at the stage door? Were you to have accidentally discovered Wesley's secret...why, who knows to what lengths Wesley would go to protect himself? I would never have even befriended you were it not for the memories you, a budding young trickster, brought back to me of happier times..." Herbie's words gasped on.

"For years I suffered this grim existence. I wasted my talents on Wesley's brutal stage. A couple times, I tried to find other work in New York but Arnold found me, and my punishment was swift—four days down here the first time, a week the second. Once, I even tried to flee the city, but both times Arnold snared me before I even reached the train station, and I was down here for another week. After that, I resigned myself to working at Wesley Jones's cruel theater forevermore." His head sank, gray hair trailing. "That was until late yesterday afternoon when…"

"Your old friend Boris Zell left you a letter." Just one knot left.

"A miracle! Normally, Arnold checks all letters, but Boris, purely by chance, had tucked the letter inside a parcel containing a jar of his Magician's Fire, a gift to me. Arnold tore open a bit of the wrapping, assumed it was merely equipment, and let me have it. And indeed, a jar of Magician's Fire was a most welcome gift, but it was the letter, and the offer in it, which caused me most delight." Feebly, Herbie looked up.

"The thought of returning to the freedom of a life on the road again with my dear, old friend Boris by my side…why, it awakened hopes and desires that I simply could not contain. Despite Wesley, despite that tyrannical trapeze artist, I foolishly decided to risk it all one final time…"

"You decided to escape after the performance last

night!" Two fingernails gripped the last loop of knot. "Was that why you looked so strange when we saw you before the show? You must have just received Boris's note! You were trembling and pale and…"

"Of course I was! I was terrified! But I was also determined, fool that I am. I packed my bags. I didn't say a word to a soul. I cleared my room of all props and equipment I might need to take with me. My feeble hope was to sneak out through the front of the theater while Arnold was distracted at the stage door. He always liked to show off there with Wesley after a performance—"

"But Wesley sent him up to find you! So…" Just a couple strands remained, but they were stubbornly intertwined. "But I was watching your dressing room. I saw what happened! And the man I saw with you was big, Herbie. Not thin like Arnold."

"The slant of the light, boy." Herbie shook his head. "Any decent magician would tell you that a shadow cast upon a window is far larger than its source. No, it was Arnold all right. He burst in just as I was about to leave—the trapeze artist's grip had me once again!" More tears trickled along the wrinkles. "I was forced to the ground, and I heard him scream his master's words…"

"What's yours is mine and always shall be! You remember that, Herbie Lemster!" Harry repeated the words as his fingernails worked the final strands.

"He forced me to the floor! Desperate, I thought of all I would miss, of a life with my dear friend Boris. The sheer misery gave me the strength to fight back the only way I could. With—"

"Boris's jar of Magician's Fire! You threw it at Arnold. It exploded and—"

"Smoke everywhere! The window shattered! Arnold was thrown to the ground and knocked his head, and for a few seconds, I thought I might be free. What madness!" The tears overflowed the wrinkles, seeping across Herbie's face. "But even through the purple mist, he found me. Out of my dressing room I was bundled—"

"And the other performers saw you. Of course they did!" The final strand broke loose, and the ropes slithered away. "But they were too terrified to say anything. They knew the same thing would happen to them."

"Along the corridor, into Wesley's office..." The last remnants of strength faded from Herbie's voice. "Down, down, down here..."

It all made sense. Harry hurled the ropes away. No

magical disappearance—just the brutal bundling of a feeble old man down a corridor. Bruno the Strongman and all the others had sworn they hadn't seen a thing, but only because they were as terrified as Herbie. As for everyone who had searched the theater—who would have thought to look beneath the mantelpiece in Wesley Jones's office or have had fingers nimble enough to detect that hidden switch? Weak from being tied so long, Herbie slithered off the chair into the water. Harry grabbed the old man's arm, pulled him up, and together they stumbled out of the cage.

"Don't worry, Herbie. I'll rescue you!"

"But how? How will you do that…"

"I'll get you out of here for a start!"

"All on your own? But…what about young Billie? And Arthur? They are waiting to help, perhaps?"

"Not really…" Harry realized that, for some time now, he hadn't had the slightest thought of his friends.

"But why? You are always together, the three of you!" The old man's voice sounded strangely hysterical. "You don't mean to say you came here alone?"

"Well, yes…"

"At least tell me they know where you are. You told them, didn't you?"

"I don't think so…"

"Stop right there, shoeshine boy!" said a familiar voice.

Harry looked up even as Herbie slithered out of his grasp and dropped back into the water. There, standing at the bottom of the stairway, were Wesley Jones and Arnold.

Chapter 20

EVERYTHING HERBIE HAD SAID about Arnold's strength was true. With a single lopsided stride, the stage manager was on Harry, his spindly limbs locking him in a hold. Harry fought back, but every move was blocked by a steely hand, and he realized that he was upside down, the water and the iron steps flying underneath him as he was effortlessly carried up the stairs. A flash of light and he was back in Wesley's office. The slam of a cupboard door and it was dark again.

"Thought you'd help out ol' Herbie, did ya? And all the other no-good performing folk who work here, I'll be bound! Well, you ain't doing no such thing. Me and Mr. Jones, we're who decides what goes on around here. Now don't you say a word, boy!"

A bony hand over Harry's mouth made sure of that. Arnold had slammed himself in the cupboard too, but his face could just be made out in the gloom, those normally wide-open eyes tightened into narrow slits, staring furiously. Harry stared back. His heart was pounding faster than he had ever known. It felt like a knife, jabbing into him with every beat.

Billie and Arthur. He saw them, their blurred faces as they tumbled together down the fire escape. Desperately, his mind flew back over that strange, muddled conversation again, thinking of every word that had been spoken, of every tiny gesture that had been made. Had he said anything about where he was going? *No, nothing at all.* As far as Billie and Arthur were concerned, he was just off on another bit of the investigation. They would have no idea…

That he needed their help very badly indeed.

"I daresay you know I ain't been so pleased with you, Herbie." Footsteps, and Wesley's voice was heard through the cupboard door. "A day in the Punishment Chamber tends to make people aware of how I see 'em."

"Yes, Mr. Jones…" Herbie's broken voice managed a few words.

"But I never stay in a funk for too long." A well-oiled clunk as the mantelpiece swiveled shut. "That boy wasted his time in so many ways. I was always intending to release you around now. Why, I need my star act to take the stage again...*don't I?*"

The thud of a plump fist on a desk. From Herbie, a wheeze.

"Yes, Mr. Jones! Of course!"

"Now, that boy. Friend of yours, is he?"

"Yes..."

"He's going to have a lucky escape. As we speak, that very boy is running as fast as he can down the street outside, our stage manager right after him. Arnold'll give him a fair licking, but he'll let him go. 'Course he will. Friend or not, I don't think that boy's gonna be troubling us again, do you, Herbie?"

"No, Mr. Jones... Thank you..."

Herbie's voice was a gasp of fear but also of relief. But Harry knew something far worse than a licking was in store for him, and he fought against Arnold's grip with even greater force, his heart jabbing so hard that his eyes watered with pain. His muscles strained, his limbs tried to wriggle their way out of Arnold's grip, and his mind was wriggling even faster, going through those last moments on the fire escape.

They won't even have been surprised, he thought. *It's not as if they're not used to me running off, is it?* In the cupboard's darkness, Harry felt his face burn again as he thought of everything that had happened. The hurled umbrella. The smashed pieces of porcelain. Worst of all, Arthur's outburst on the fire escape. *"Enough of that in my life already..."* Harry shook his head from side to side, but the memory of those words stayed in there, painfully lodged.

The cupboard door flew open. Herbie was gone, and Harry was out of the cupboard, Arnold's trapeze artist limbs still wrapped around him. The mantelpiece slid open on its hinges. Harry fought, but Arnold bundled him back into the dark. The candle stub flickered, the black water rippled, the cage door slid shut with Harry inside. He flung himself against the iron bars. He pried at the lock. His eyes flicked about, his fingers twitched, as a tiny part of him wondered if he could play that little game, the one where he searched out some stray bit of metal, one that he could bend into the correct shape to pick a lock. But he wasn't going to find any bit of stray metal, was he? *Not trapped here in a water-filled cage.* Staring at the spiral staircase, he saw Wesley Jones making his way down, rotating his pink top hat between his thumbs.

"The Punishment Chamber is my usual name for this place." Wesley was at the foot of the stairs. His face was as plump as ever, but the lips were slightly apart and the teeth behind were surprisingly sharp. "You interfered with my theater, boy. Do you have any idea how hard it is, running a theatrical establishment in this city? Many would say I manage things the only sensible way."

"You told me Herbie was happy!" Harry heard a voice ring out, unusually high-pitched, and could hardly believe it was his own. "You said he was a friend of yours for ten years! You said he and all the other performers love working here but—"

"Sure, I lied." The lips revealed a few more teeth. "You haven't been in New York very long, have you?"

A lever clanked. Arnold was next to the foot of the stairs, knee-deep in water, and he was tugging a lever while making various adjustments to it with one of the wrenches from his leather bag. Another clank and water flooded out of the various pipes that sprawled around the room's clammy walls. Churning, the black water began circling the cage. And it wasn't just circling, Harry noticed.

It was rising.

"You didn't really believe that you, a mere boy, could bring down the Wesley Jones Theater?" The pink hat twirled once more. "A theater which I, an experienced vaudevillian, have engineered to operate with precision. Patiently, expertly, I have broken my performers' spirits, while carefully preserving all that makes them so valuable, namely, their skills. Less a theater, more an ingeniously assembled machine—and I am powerfully proud of it. The idea that you could bring such careful work crashing down is absurd."

"I'll tell everyone what you're doing!" Harry heard that high-pitched voice again.

"Well, yes, that *might* bring it all crashing down." Wesley put his head to one side, as if finding the idea genuinely intriguing. "But my point still stands because there is no chance whatsoever of you doing that, shoeshine boy." He nodded at Arnold. "The second lever, Arnold."

"Right away, Mr. Jones!" Arnold held up another wrench, loped up the stairs, and went to work.

"As I mentioned before, the Punishment Chamber is my usual name for this contraption." Wesley turned back. "Every now and then, however, a different title is needed. Wesley's Whirlpool, that's what I call it then."

Halfway up the stairs, Arnold grabbed another lever. He twirled the wrench, loosened a bolt, and crunched the lever down. The whole staircase shuddered, and in the middle of the swirling, rising water, the cage shuddered too.

"I never liked that boy, Mr. Jones!" Arnold dropped the wrench back into his bag, sneering. "Remember how he talked to me about being such a great fan of the theater? Dreams of being a performer himself, I'll be bound."

"Ah, but it is one thing to dream of a life upon the stage, and another thing to achieve such a life!" Wesley nodded. "Or, in the case of this boy, to hang onto any life at all."

The cage was still shuddering. The bars were throbbing, and when Harry gripped them, they turned his fists to white blurs. Something directly under his feet thudded, and the cage began to grind downward.

"Now, I daresay, theatrical fellow that you are, you are expecting this machine to be a spectacular one. A fanciful contraption against which you can pit your wits—deadly piranhas or electric eels, perhaps? I'm sorry to disappoint you. This machine is merely a plumbing device." Wesley headed back up the stairs.

"All theaters, no matter how carefully run, require occasional cleaning. Once in a while, they get clogged, if you like, by an unwanted item, a foreign body— something that needs to be flushed out. You, my boy, are such an item, and Wesley's Whirlpool is the plumbing tool that will flush you away, while Arnold and I attend to a far more important affair—the preparation of this evening's show.

"The cage you are in is moving downward and the water, you will have noticed, is swirling upward in whirlpool-like style. I am sure you understand the result regarding yourself. Afterward, sluices will open, and this room and all its contents—including those that remain in the cage—will sweep straight out to the Hudson River and flow away from this great city of ours toward the sea."

"You can't do this!"

"Is that what you think? You really *haven't* been in New York for long." Wesley returned his hat to his head. "Nor, by the process I have just described, will you be for very much longer."

He trod up the stairs and, together with Arnold, disappeared into the gloom.

Chapter 21

HARRY FLUNG HIMSELF AT the bars. He pulled at them and kicked them, but the cage kept grinding steadily down. *Think of something.* He watched the cage's lock sink below the surface, ducked down, and peered at it in the watery darkness. Was there a chance, the ghost of a chance, that he might be able to find some bit of metal after all? Something to bend into a pick? *Impossible.* The only metal was the cage itself, welded and bolted together.

Beneath its base, Harry made out a steadily turning iron cog, its teeth levering the contraption downward. Reaching through the bars, he tried to stop it with his fingers, but the teeth tore through his skin, and a trembling bubble flew out of his mouth, a shout of pain. He burst back to the surface, his hand bleeding. His body cold and numb, he could no longer feel his heart jabbing. He just shuddered as it slammed against the inside of his chest.

Billie and Arthur. He saw their faces again, hovering in the blackness. *What would they be doing now if they had any idea what was happening?* he thought, and he knew the answer immediately. Despite everything, they would be racing across Manhattan and making up a plan, and it would be a good one too. He could see them now, their determined expressions, and he could hear their voices...

He heard other sounds as well, the clatter of plates and spoons, and even more strangely, he felt a patch of warmth on each of his hands, even as they gripped the icy bars. He saw his friends again. They were at a table now, the one in that grimy diner, crumbs of chocolate sponge cake scattering on the cloth. Billie and Arthur were holding each other's hands, and they were holding the hands of their other friend, the one across the table...

The one who they'll never see again.

The water was up to his chest. He ducked back under it and reached for the cog again, but the teeth tore through his skin even faster this time. Another bubble of pain, and he shot back up out of the water, so fast that his head hit the bars at the top of the cage. He gripped them, and the vibrations shuddered through his bones.

One last time, he saw Billie and Arthur. They were back sitting at the bottom of that fire escape, the Princess Moldo costume in ruins, the dress ripped, the bonnet squashed. Why, thanks to him, Billie had even lost the very best bit of it, the Princess Moldo spectacles, genuinely made in Peru and knocked off by his arm during the fall down the fire escape.

The Princess Moldo spectacles.

Harry's hand flew under the water. He dug inside his jacket, the pocket to the left. The spectacles were still there, where he had slid them, as he rattled away on the streetcar. He hadn't thought about them much then, apart from deciding he would give them back to his friends when he could. But he was thinking about them now. He had never thought about anything so intently in his life.

He lifted them up. The dark lenses were smashed; the frames were bent. But the thin arms were still intact.

Arms with curved, bendable metal ends.

Harry sucked in another gulp of air and dove under the water. He tore off one of the spectacle arms and sank toward the iron cog. With his still-bleeding hand, he angled the curved length of metal between the teeth and watched it catch hold. The cage shuddered to halt, although the spectacle arm wouldn't hold long and the water was still rising. But he had won himself a few more seconds, and he shot to the surface, grabbed another gasp of air, and sank back down to the lock. In his hands, Harry was already testing the strength of the remaining spectacle arm to see how easily it would bend.

Could it work? For the Great Train Escape, he had picked the padlock with a nail held between his teeth. He had picked the lock on the library door with a paper clip, and he had picked his way into the hotel manager's office with a fork. But what if the lock on the cage door was unusually difficult? What if the made-in-Peru spectacle arm was too weak to hold the shape? Even worse, it was almost impossible to see in the watery gloom, and Harry could hardly make out the lock's insides.

Using a little guesswork, he twisted the spectacle arm into a new curve. It slid in, and he probed the lock's levers but gave up because his hand was trembling too much. His breath was out, and his heart was making his whole body shake. *Grab another breath and try again*, he decided, and he pushed for the water's surface.

Too late. The water had risen too high, and his face slammed against the cage bars. His lips strained upwards, but the rippling surface was too far away. He sank downward, his heart throbbing, his legs, arms, and hands losing their last traces of feeling. The water became darker, more blurry, as his eyelids flickered. The Princess Moldo spectacle arm slid from his fingers. He hung there in the water, icy and black.

His eyes closed. He stopped moving.

One...one...one last try...

An eye opened. He peered down and saw the spectacle arm just vanishing into the gloom. His fingers twitched after it, but it was already gone. With a last quiver of strength, he turned himself in the water, reaching after it. Slowly, he rotated until he was nearly upside down...

With the tip of his fingers, he caught it.

Still upside down, he saw the lock. It was just a few feet away. Feebly, he lifted the spectacle arm. He tried to angle it in, but it bumped against the keyhole's edges. Then it slid in. He tilted it, twisted it. He had to concentrate on keeping his numb hands moving, stopping them from falling limply away. His eyes were wide open, unblinking, but the water was growing darker and more blurry. He could hardly see at all.

But he could hear.

And, muffled by water, he heard…

…*a click.*

The lock sprang open. Harry tugged the door, but it was stiff, so he had to tug again. It slid across, and he tried to squeeze through, but the gap was too narrow, and he had to wriggle. He wondered if he had already died, if the whole experience of the last few seconds had just been the final flickers of his drowning mind—then a kick sent him racing upward and he burst through the surface.

Air raced into his lungs so fast that it was as if he had been punched, and he nearly sank back into the water with the shock. He struggled on, reached the stairs, and pulled himself up them, gasping, his hands still empty of feeling. Reaching the top, he slammed into a solid wall, the back of the mantelpiece, but he remembered the position of the switch on the other side and found the mechanism. He sprang it, toppled into Wesley's office, thudded onto the rug, and realized what a terrible mistake he had made.

Footsteps. Uneven footsteps, echoing up the corridor outside the office.

Harry tried to get up. His fingers arched on the rug, trying to push, but his strength was gone. The footsteps were closer now. *What a fool*, he thought, not to realize that Wesley or Arnold might return to the office. His escape had been for nothing, even with the help of his friends…

His friends.

"Harry!"

Arthur had slid out from behind the office door. Billie had thrown aside a curtain. They stared at him, but then they swung around in the direction of the footsteps. Arthur sprang toward the mantelpiece, and Harry heard the grind as it slid shut. He felt Billie's hands under his arms, tugging him up, and Arthur was helping her too, dragging him out through the office door. The footsteps were even louder, and Arnold's shadow slanted into view, but Billie flung open another door, bundled them into a cobweb-strewn dressing room, and silently closed the door behind them.

More footsteps. The sound of papers fluttering on Wesley's desk. Billie tweaked the dressing door open just a crack, and Harry saw the shape of Arnold, papers under his arm, standing in the doorway to Wesley's office. He was staring in the direction of the mantelpiece. A satisfied nod, the faintest waft of a chuckle, and the stage manager swung back off down the corridor. Harry waited until the shuffling footsteps were gone, completely gone. Then, he sputtered out the words that, from the moment he had seen his friends, had been trying to force their way out through his lips.

"I'm sorry… I'm sorry…"

Immediately, his voice gave out. His lungs still ached, his heart still pounded, and the effort of speaking nearly choked him. But nothing was going to hold him back. Gripping the dusty edge of the dressing-room counter, he gathered his breath, all the time aware of his two friends staring at him.

"Pardon?" said Arthur.

"I'm sorry about not listening to you earlier, Artie…" His breath was back, and he struggled on, in between gasps. "When you were trying to tell me all about the Princess Moldo plan…I should have listened. I know that now! Apart from anything else, you were right about having enough of that sort of thing in your life already…" He was still gasping, and he was dripping wet, but he forced himself to meet Arthur's eyes. "Last thing you want is a friend who ignores you too. So I'm sorry, Artie. I really am…"

His voice gave out again. And for a while, nothing

more was said. Arthur just stared at Harry across the dilapidated dressing room. But then the younger boy nodded, adjusted his tie, and looked away.

"Fair enough," he said.

"What about me?" said Billie, drumming her fingers on the counter.

"Well, obviously, I'm really sorry about that too." Another gasp, but Harry found that his breath came back faster this time. That was fortunate, because Billie was looking straight at him. "You're right. I should have gone along with the Princess Moldo business without interfering. In fact, I should have paid a lot more attention to you and Artie generally, I reckon." He swallowed.

"You were right earlier, Billie. Each of us, we're not so much, not on our own. Arthur's a rich boy who gets ignored. You're just a penniless street kid, and as for me, well, no one was paying me and my tricks any attention until you two came along. But once we joined together…"

"Exactly," said Billie.

"Besides, why wouldn't I want to listen to you? You're just as good at thinking up plans as I am! All those stories of the stuff you've got up to, Billie—that proves it, doesn't it? And you're good too, Artie—how could you not be, with all those books you've read! Come to think of it, both of you being here at the Wesley Jones Theater proves just how good you are. I didn't say where I was going—how'd you work it out?"

"If you'd just stop talking, we might tell you." Billie dropped into a rickety chair and swung her boots onto the dressing room counter. "It was a pretty smart business—eh, Artie?"

"Absolutely." Artie dropped into a chair too, a tiny smile beginning to curve on his lips. "It wasn't that hard, to be honest. Number 47, that was the streetcar you jumped onto."

"And we remembered you jumping onto the same number streetcar before, so we just looked up where the Number 47 went and saw it was the Wesley Jones Theater." Billie's boots swapped places. "Pretty clever, yeah?"

"Brilliant." There was no third chair, so Harry just stayed where he was, clinging to the wall. "Just brilliant."

"So we came right here and managed to break in easy enough. Sneaking up just now, we heard Wesley Jones, owner of this place, chatting to some thin guy about—"

"About a boy!" Arthur leaned back in his chair. "About how they'd 'dealt with him' and how he

194

'wouldn't be trouble no longer.' It didn't sound good, Harry!"

"No, it did not," Billie continued. "Anyway, despite everything you've done recently, Harry, we're still your pals, and someone has to look after you, so we thought we'd find out more—"

"We snuck up here to Wesley Jones's office and started searching for clues. And we'd just started doing that when the mantelpiece swung open and you came in!"

"Exactly. So that's what we've been up to. What about you?" Billie peered at her friend and studied the water trickling from his clothes, the puddle spreading around his boots. "Been swimming?"

Harry told them. He was still recovering, so the first part was a bit of a muddle, but he kept going, forcing out as many words as he could. He told them about Boris, about Herbie, about the terrible truth behind Wesley Jones's theater. He must have been making some sort of sense, because his friends were saying nothing at all, taking everything in. Harry saw Arthur's mouth fall open, and even Billie showed not the slightest sign of interrupting. She stayed that way until Harry reached the bit about stumbling back into the office and collapsing on the rug.

"He tried to kill you? Actually, properly *kill* you?"

"The Cruel Theater of Wesley Jones!" Arthur whistled. "Who would have believed it?"

"And who's gonna believe it even *now*?" Billie was up, out of the chair, pacing the room, twiddling her thumbs behind her so fast that they seemed to propel her along. "That's the trouble, Artie!"

She's right. Harry was still dripping wet, but he was feeling stronger now, and he could see what Billie was saying. Yes, he had discovered the terrible truth behind Herbie's disappearance. Yes, Wesley Jones had tried to silence him forever, not one to take chances. *But that doesn't mean telling the world the truth about this terrible theater is going to be easy*, he reflected—as Billie was continuing to point out.

"It would have been fine if you'd got Herbie out—he could back us up. But he's still trapped here, isn't he? He'll be too scared to say a word! Same for all the performers! So that leaves just us, a bunch of kids—and it's just like you said before, Harry. No one's going to take our word for it. Not the police, not anyone else. At most, someone might ask Wesley a few questions, but do you think he'll have any trouble thinking up something to cover his tracks? Not one bit! It's a hard one all right…" Her thumbs twiddled even faster. "Mind you, I'm not saying it's impossible…"

Definitely not impossible. Leaning against the dressing room's crumbling wall, Harry realized that little bits and pieces of a plan were flying around in his thoughts, waiting to be put together so that this business could be sorted out once and for all. They were getting clearer all the time, those bits and pieces, and yet he decided to ignore them completely, just for now.

He felt his eyes narrow and his teeth grit with the concentration of doing so. Given everything that had happened recently, it seemed important that he approach things a bit differently this time. He let his eyes open and glanced down at his left fist to remind himself why.

Knuckles white, it was still clutching the twisted remains of the Princess Moldo spectacles. Slowly, he turned to his friends and spoke.

"Let's do this together, shall we?"

Chapter 22

Harry hid in the backstage shadows, Billie squeezed next to him, Arthur huddled behind. Out on the stage, the evening show was underway. Bruno the Strongman had just finished his act and was loping toward the wings with a mournful expression. *But all the performers look miserable*, thought Harry—the pearl-diving dancers, the juggling acrobats, the man who told jokes while dressed as a parrot. *Why wouldn't they, with nothing but a desperate future of slaving at the Cruel Theater of Wesley Jones awaiting them?* Screwing his eye to the tiny hole in the backstage wall, Harry peered out at the audience and listened to the excited muttering.

"Herbie Lemster! He's back, and no one knows how!"

"The police never solved it. It's a darn mystery!"

"I was there that night. Vanished into a puff of smoke, he did!"

"Dark forces, that's what they say! It's the only explanation."

The rumors raced about. They built in volume until they almost blotted out the applause that accompanied the next act, the juggling acrobats. The audience settled down to watch, but clearly, from their faces and the continued muttering, they were thinking only of Herbie Lemster, due to appear at any moment.

"Wesley's plan's working nicely, ain't it, Harry?" Billie peered through another hole.

"Certainly is," Harry muttered. "Arnold's slapped up a few posters outside announcing Herbie's return. Plus, I saw Wesley wandering about the audience just before the show, chatting and laughing—"

"Getting the rumors started!" Arthur butted in. "He's told the newspapers too—plenty of journalists in the audience. I saw them come in. All of New York has been talking about Herbie, and now he's come back out of nowhere! Wesley isn't just going to keep his terrible theater going; it's going to be more successful than ever and—"

"Pretty smart plan." Billie swung around from her

spy hole. "But Wesley Jones ain't the only one who's cooked up one of *those*, is he?"

She pointed at the sheet of paper in Arthur's hands. It was covered with three different types of handwriting, all spiraling in different directions, a mass of scribbled words and diagrams. It had been Artie's idea that they each write their different ideas down, and the result was something of a mess, but every last scribble had fit onto one page, and Arthur was proudly holding it in his hands. Billie reached out and took hold of a corner of it. Harry grabbed it too. It hovered there, gripped in their three hands.

"Let's just do it, shall we?"

They raced through the shadows. Unseen, they glided past Bruno, the pearl-diving ladies, and a couple of the Cossack dancers, all looking as down-trodden as ever. Arriving in the corner of the backstage area by the huge piece of wooden seaweed, Harry rooted through the collection of ropes, chose one, tossed it into Arthur's arms, and headed off with him into the dark. Hurrying through the gloom, he spotted the most mournful-looking figure of all, trudging toward the stage.

Herbie. What a broken man he looked to be. His gray hair drooped, his body shivered, and his suit was still damp and creased after his time imprisoned in Wesley Jones's cage. Harry remembered the terror of the old magician down there, and he looked hardly less frightened now, tottering through the wings, forced to perform once again. A dreadful sight, made even more terrible by the sound of a familiar voice wafting gleefully from the stage.

"Ladies and gentlemen, we come now to the main business of the evening. The miraculous return of Herbie Lemster, our resident magician!" It was Wesley Jones, out on the stage, the pink top hat twirling as he boomed out his announcement. "Many of you may have heard of the strange events of last night. Purple smoke, an inexplicable disappearance! Sadly, ladies and gentleman, I am unable to shed any light on the affair. It will be a mystery that will grip and baffle this city for years to come, I venture."

A wink over the hat's rim. "What I can say is, however unexplained his disappearance, Herbie is with us once again. Puzzle for yourselves, if you will, about his vanishing. But here he is, ladies and gentlemen! *Here he is!*"

The applause was tumultuous. The audience cheered, and there were even shrieks as the old magician went shuffling on. Harry was deep in the backstage gloom, but he could still make out the stage—and he had never seen anyone look as miserable as Herbie taking up his position, nor had he ever seen anyone as gleefully happy as Wesley Jones as he marched into the wings. Chuckling, the theater manager handed his hat to Arnold, who was smirking and also looked pleased about the business.

Harry shifted his gaze to Billie, as she wandered out of the shadows and strolled up to the two villains.

"Excuse me?" She propped herself casually against some scenery. "Don't suppose you've seen a boy around here, have you? Harry's his name, and he's a good friend of mine—"

Arnold lunged for her, and Billie was running as fast as she could. Harry watched her tiny outline hurtling away from the wings toward him. Arnold and Wesley were close behind, but Billie raced through the dark, her glue-spattered smock flapping as she gathered speed. What would she call this latest adventure of hers when she told the story? The Wesley Jones Theater Dash, maybe? Harry watched her speed past him, vanishing through a doorway into the props room, which was where they had carefully agreed she should run.

Even though it was a dead end.

"You won't get out that way, kid!"

Harry saw Wesley and Arnold, their faces grinning as they closed in on the doorway. He heard Billie scrabbling about in the props-crammed room. *Caught in a trap.* But who was? Billie or them?

"Ready, Harry?"

"Ready!"

A rope was pulled tight across the doorway, level with Arnold's and Wesley's knees. Harry held one end, while Arthur gripped the other on the opposite side. The two men slammed onto the props room floor, and Billie skipped over them, not particularly seeming to mind as she trod on Wesley's hat, squashing it pancake flat, and on Arnold's hand, producing a high-pitched yell. She was out of the room. Still clutching either end of the rope, Arthur and Harry slammed and locked the door.

"All went rather smoothly," Arthur said.

"Nice work," Billie agreed.

"Ready for the next part, Artie?" said Harry.

"I'll just finish off a few rewrites," Artie muttered, flipping over the sheet of paper and jotting some more as they hurried back toward the stage. Applause roared as Herbie completed the first part of his act. Harry could see him out there, his frail arms holding up the glittering knives that had been magically hurled at him, his face staring sadly as the audience howled. A miserable sight.

But with a jab of his pencil, Arthur was ready, and Harry unhooked the rope that held the curtain, sending it thundering down. The audience gasped with dismay, and Arthur and Billie marched onto the stage, leaving Harry waiting in the backstage darkness.

"Ladies and gentlemen, I have an announcement to make!" This was Arthur's big moment, and Harry watched him leap to the front, the sheet of paper fluttering in his hand. "Fear not, Herbie's act is not over! Indeed, it has only just begun. Never in your life will you have witnessed…"

"Who are you?"

"Get off the stage!"

"Kids! What're two kids doing up there?"

A tricky start, thought Harry. But his friends had expected that. And it wasn't as if anyone was actually going to stop them, was it? From his position in the wings, Harry glanced around and saw the other performers standing there, too astonished to do anything, while all that could be heard of Arnold and Wesley was some faraway hammering on a door. Meanwhile, out on the stage, Billie was nudging Artie, keeping him going.

"Ladies and gentlemen, prepare yourself for the shock of your lives! You will not be seeing Herbie's usual tricks. No poisonous spiders and flowers! No bicycling over deadly spikes! No, what you are about to witness is more startling by far! For you are about to see with your own eyes, hear with your own ears…" Arthur yelled the last few words at the very top of his voice. "*The truth behind the disappearance of Herbie Lemster!* A tale of trickery, malice, and attempted murder!"

Silence. *Nicely timed*, Harry thought, and he saw that Arthur looked pleased too, folding his speech up and sliding it into his pocket with a tap. A few more seconds went by and still not a sound from the crowd. Even before the show, they had been obsessed with rumors of Herbie's vanishing. *That'll be nothing compared to now*, Harry decided, and darted through a doorway, running up a corridor that ran parallel to the auditorium.

"If you want to find out more, follow us!" Billie's voice echoed through the theater. Passing a doorway, Harry glanced back through it and saw his friends leaping from the stage. Another doorway, and he saw the two of them running up the aisle through the audience, who seemed trapped in silence, gaping at them.

But then Harry heard a seat thudding up, followed by another and another. Behind his friends, he saw members of the audience, all around the auditorium, stumbling toward the aisle.

"The secret of Herbie's disappearance? Tell us!"

"What is it? I demand to know!"

"Is it dark magic? Like everyone says it is?"

"Follow them! Don't let them get away!"

Harry took off again. He slammed into the foyer and flung open the door that led up to Wesley's office. Racing upstairs, he heard Billie and Arthur's voices echoing behind him, along with hundreds of other voices, a thundering wall of shouts and gasps and demands for information. *They won't be disappointed,* he thought, as he flew along a final corridor, slammed into the office, rummaged under the mantelpiece shelf, and sent the marble bulk lurching to the side.

He leaped through into the dark. Flying down the spiral stairs, he splashed into the icy water. Over by the wall, he tugged at a lever, making the water swirl, and then he waded toward the cage. He slid the door open and slammed it shut behind himself. A flick of his wrist sent the key flying from the lock, plopping into the water, far away. Harry felt his heart throb with the memory of his last experience with this terrible device but ignored it. He grabbed the end of a rope that he had positioned earlier, running all the way over to the lever by the stairs, and tugged it. The lever clanked to the left and the cage began grinding down into the swirling black water again.

"Behold, we are in the office of Wesley Jones himself!" Harry heard Billie's voice, close now. "The respectable theater manager. But all is not as it seems!"

"Out of our way!"

The crowd was clattering down the stairs, the darkness echoing with their cries. Mouths fell open, eyes bulged, and a lady near the front fainted but was picked up and carried along. The entire staircase groaned as more than a hundred people peered around the gloomy place, with its throbbing pipes, swirling water, and single flickering candle.

"What is this place?"

"Look at the speed of that water!"

"Who would build something like this?"

"In a theater of all places!"

"What's that over there? It's…a cage!"

"It's *moving*!"

"Sinking, you mean!"

"And there's someone in it!"

"A *boy*!"

The darkness shuddered with their screams. The crowd was in the water, surrounding the cage, yelling at it, pulling at its bars. Harry spotted Billie and Arthur in the water too, screaming loudest of all, all part of the plan to create the most panicked atmosphere possible. Harry saw the rigid faces, the screaming mouths. The cage kept grinding down. The water was up to his neck, but hidden beneath its surface his fingers were reaching for that snapped-off arm of the Princess Moldo spectacles...

"Save him! Save him!"

"Stop the machine!"

"Who put him in there? Who would do such a thing?"

"What about the theater owner? It was his office up there, wasn't it?"

"Just get the boy out!"

"I can't! It's locked!"

"Stop it sinking someone! Stop it!"

"Look!"

The cage door slammed open. Harry shot up through the foaming water, gasping for air. Two more ladies fainted, collapsing on the stairs, but no one noticed, too astounded at the sight of Harry clambering out of the water and onto the top of the cage. They also seemed astounded by the words that raced out of his dripping mouth.

"It's time for you to know the truth…about Wesley Jones!"

Again, the story flew out of him. The last time he had told it, he had been recovering in the cobweb-strewn dressing room, and it had been a bit of a muddle. But the words racing out of him now were far clearer. Carefully, precisely, he had been prepared by Arthur, who had jotted down exactly what he should say so the whole affair would be presented in the easiest way possible. Harry had memorized every word and, from the look of the audience's faces as he reached the speech's end, those words were having the desired effect.

"And so, Wesley Jones imprisoned me. He left me here to die! But I escaped! I escaped, and here I am now to tell the truth of Herbie Lemster's disappearance…and of the Cruel Theater of Wesley Jones!"

"Wesley Jones! Stage Manager Arnold! Find them!"

The water churned, and the iron stairs shuddered as the crowd raced out of the dungeon. Harry jumped off the cage and was swept along by the jostling bodies. He saw that the same thing was happening to his friends. Together, they hurtled along with the furious crowd as it poured out into Wesley's office and surged back into the theater, all the way to the props room, where, as Harry's speech had made clear, Wesley and Arnold had been so cleverly imprisoned.

"They've gone!"

"Smashed their way out!"

"Used a palm tree as a battering ram!"

The door hung off its hinges, and one of the larger props, a fake tropical plant, lay nearby, snapped in half. Standing around were the various performers—Bruno the Strongman, the Cossack dancers, the juggling acrobats, the man who told jokes—looking confused. But most confused of all was the small, frail figure standing with them.

Herbie Lemster. His eyes were wide, taking in the scene before him. He was staring at the smashed-down door. He was staring at the crowd. His legs were weak, but his fellow performers kept him upright. When he spoke, it was clear he could hardly believe what he was saying.

"They have fled!" the old magician gasped. "Just a minute ago. None of us knew what was happening! They smashed through the door and raced up toward Mr. Jones's office—but they came racing down again when they heard you coming." Bewildered, he pointed at the stage door, which was still rocking on its hinges.

"Ran off into the night! None of us could make head or tail of it…"

"Catch them! Bring them back!"

A section of the crowd broke away and swept out through the stage door. But Harry paid no attention to that. Instead, his gaze was fixed on Herbie. He was still unsteady on his feet, his face was still wearily wrinkled, and yet it seemed, from what he was saying, that he was finally starting to understand what had just happened.

"You mean to say…we're free?" Tears trickled down his face. "Free from our dreaded owner and his terrible trapeze artist stage manager? Free of the Cruel Theater of Wesley Jones? It's not possible. And yet… it is! Thanks to…"

The crowd gasped. Herbie had lifted a trembling hand, and for a moment it seemed as if he was about to perform some magical act. But instead, Herbie just extended a finger. Tears flooding, he faced the crowd, pointing in the direction of Harry and his friends.

"Thanks to these remarkable young people here! This boy. His friends too. They've set us performers free, ladies and gentlemen! *Free!*"

The crowd was out of control. Hands gripped Harry, and he rose into the air. Glancing across, he saw Billie being held aloft too, and Arthur. Then the throwing began, the hands beneath Harry and his friends powering them up into the air and catching them again, while the whole theater throbbed with cheers. *Heroes, all three of us*, thought Harry, as the crowd threw them higher and higher. And Billie and Arthur's twists and turns in midair, he noticed, were every bit as spectacular as his own.

"We did it!" Billie waved at him as she flew upward again.

"We really did!" shouted Arthur, his tie flying wildly around him.

"The Rescue of Herbie Lemster!" Harry yelled back. "It really is our most spectacular trick yet!"

He gazed around at the crowd's faces, whooping, cheering. And he noticed one face toward the back. White hair, white eyebrows, a pair of staring eyes. Harry thought nothing of it, but found himself looking at the face a second time, and a third time too.

I've seen him before.

He looked more closely. The man wore a pale, neatly tailored suit, and his hair was perfectly white. Otherwise, there was no reason to pick him out. But Harry kept staring, as he flew up and down.

The tightrope walk at the Hotel Crosby. He had

glimpsed the man then. A flash of paleness in the windowpane, a face, white hair, a piercing stare. Harry couldn't be absolutely sure, but the longer he looked, the surer he became. It was the same man—but what was he doing here in the crowd at the Wesley Jones Theater? The Hotel Crosby was on the other side of town. Why would he be in both places, with just a few hours in between? As if this wasn't odd enough, why was the pale-suited man making notes? He was scribbling in a leather notebook, which appeared to have some sort of white bird on the cover. Even more strangely, wisps of white mist seemed to be rising from the pages…

Harry tried to look closer. But the crowd cheered even louder and threw him so high in the air that he spun around. When he landed, he was facing in the other direction.

And when he looked back, the man in the pale suit was gone.

Chapter 23

T HE MAN SLID OUT through the stage door and hurried down the dark Manhattan street.

His pale suit fluttered as his long legs carried him along at high speed. His steps were perfectly regular, and the soles of his polished shoes hit the sidewalk noiselessly, neatly.

The street was dark apart from a gas lamp's flickers. But the man's eyes tracked every one of those flickers, studying the complicated shapes of every shadow they threw. His eyes swiveled about, checking the reflective surfaces of windows, metal railings, puddles on the sidewalk, for any information they might provide. The man was walking even faster now, but those eyes simply sped up, monitoring the surroundings flying past with even greater care.

He swung to the left. He marched up some steps and pushed through a heavy, gleaming door. Those polished shoes snapped over a marble floor, a chandelier glittering above. The man spiraled up a mahogany staircase, his palm just touching the balustrade, skimming beside him. He reached the top, opened another door, and walked to a desk on which a telephone stood.

His hand lifted the receiver. On the underside of his wrist, a pulse twitched. As the receiver rose past the man's neck, a further pulse could be seen twitching just above his collar. The telephone crackled to life.

"A candidate," he said. "Three of them, I now believe. I have been conducting my research with care."

More crackling. The man listened and spoke.

"I quite agree. Clearly, we need to test them. That is critical. We need to select an investigation suitable to their skills without delay and…"

The crackling went on for quite some time. Complicated pops and buzzes interwove, and the pale-suited man's eyes narrowed, as if he was deciphering complex code. But at last the crackling ceased, and he spoke again.

"Very well. I shall begin the preparations."

Chapter 24

T IME TO ESCAPE FROM *Wesley Jones's deadly device once again.*

Harry stood before the cage. Hands tore through his clothes, removed his boots, explored his mouth, searching for the tiniest hint of anything that might assist him. The hands hoisted him up and dropped him into the cage. The lid clanged down, and the key soared into the gloom. Harry saw faces in the darkness, hundreds of them, distorted with fear, thrill, and glee. But he concentrated on Billie's face, pushing up to the bars.

"Ready?"

"Like always."

A rope hoisted the cage upward. Arthur stood at the front of the stage, his arms swirling as he addressed the crowd. Swinging around to the small cluster of invited audience members, he politely asked if the search they had just conducted had revealed anything suspicious. Heads shook. Arthur flung out an arm, and the cage, a little smaller than Wesley's original, swung over a water-filled vat. Harry tightened his grip on the bars. The audience bayed, but then their noise vanished as the cage plunged into the vat. Water engulfed Harry, the cage's locked lid solid over his head.

Concentrate.

His fingers flexed. His left foot rose. The earring was lodged between two of his toes. Billie had let it fall from her ear as their faces grew close, and the toes of Harry's left foot, stripped of sock and boot, had gathered it up. It was in his hands now, bending into shape, diving into the lock. Too bad about the Princess Moldo spectacles, but the metal arms had weakened too much, and anyway, the earring was much smaller and easier to pass. As the lock sprang loose, he clanged open the lid. Clambering out, he dropped onto the stage and lowered himself in the usual bow, while Billie and Arthur ran to join him.

"Behold! He has escaped once more!" Arthur finished off his speech. "Doomed to a watery grave! Yet he has survived to tell the truth about Wesley Jones!"

The new trick. The idea for it had hit all three of them at the same time. The whole of New York was talking about the amazing rescue of Herbie Lemster, so why not let them see it unfold, night after night? As the applause roared, Harry took in the stage. To the left loomed a painted flat of Herbie's dressing-room window, from which the disappearance itself was staged with a puff of purple smoke. Forty feet high, a rope spanned the stage, on which Harry reenacted the walk into Hotel Crosby, and then there was the cage and water-filled vat, a practical way of staging the investigation's climax in Wesley Jones's deadly chamber. Best of all, there were Billie and Arthur, who helped him with every aspect of this dazzling show, Billie managing the tricks and Arthur narrating from his own script. Regarding Arthur, there was something else too, something that had only been added to the show in the last couple of performances, but which was going down very well indeed.

"Behold the latest escape…" Arthur was shouting it out as grandly as he could. "Of Harry *Houdini*!"

The new name. It had been suggested by that conversation with Arthur, which felt like such a long time ago. An invented name to catch attention: half-borrowed from a famous French magician of the past, with a touch of Hungarian. Harry liked it, and so did his friends. Most importantly, the audience seemed to like it too.

"Houdini! Houdini! Houdini!"

The name thundered out of the auditorium's gloom. Harry bowed to the cheering audience again, and on either side of him, Billie and Arthur took bows too. Then they swapped places, Billie taking the central bow, then Arthur, then Harry again. The applause swelled, the curtain fell, and the three friends headed off into the wings.

"That new curtain call works well, I think." Harry led the way up.

"You bet!" Billie snatched up her ukulele and picked out a tune. "Only fair we all get a turn!"

"Which fits in well with how things are these days at the Herbie Lemster Theater, don't you think?" said Arthur, as they reached the top of the stairs.

A quick knock, and they swept into the office. The marble mantelpiece was still there, but new bolts fixed it to the wall and a fire crackled comfortingly in its grate. More comforting still was the sight, across the desk, of Herbie Lemster, writing in a ledger and sipping a cup of tea. His gray hair was neatly combed, he was wearing a brand-new suit, and the wrinkles of his face were arranged in a cheerful expression as he greeted Harry and his friends.

"Come in! Make yourselves comfortable!"

"How's business, Herbie?" Harry dropped into a chair.

"Splendid! Your act in particular is going down tremendously well. Spectacular trickery! Although it's hardly surprising, given that you were taught by an expert." Herbie winked and pushed three envelopes across the desk. "Mind you, all the acts at this theater are impressive. That's why everyone gets their fair share of the takings."

"No trouble taking over the ownership, then?" Arthur inquired.

"How could there be? Legally, it still belongs to Jones, but he and his stage manager aren't coming back anytime soon. They're wanted by the police for extortion, blackmail, false imprisonment, and attempted murder. Along with various infringements of New York plumbing regulations."

"Last I heard, they were in Mexico City, scraping together a living with a street-theater act." Billie smiled. "Arnold juggles tin cans while Wesley tries to play a half-smashed-up saxophone."

"A rotten act for two rotten fellows." Herbie chuckled. "Anyway, I just did a deal with a bank. They purchased the theater on behalf of us performers and, given the publicity surrounding recent events, offered a very fair rate of interest. As long as we manage it well, we'll own the place outright in just a couple years. It'll be all of ours equally, although my fellow performers also suggested we paint my name on the front." Herbie blushed. "After all, why not take advantage of the excitement regarding my famous disappearance, eh? Wouldn't you agree, Boris?"

"Of course, dear Mr. Herbie! Of course!"

That familiar voice boomed across the office. Harry swung around and saw the burly magician stooped over a tiny table, stirring liquids in test tubes. Plumes of orange smoke rose around his face, but his expression was plain to see. Those tiny eyes twinkled, and a smile curved under that long, thin nose.

"At last, my dream is true! No more lonely life on the magician's road—I have found my home here with my oldest friend! Have I not, Herbie?"

"You have, dear Boris!" Herbie Lemster sprang from his desk and put an arm around the hefty figure.

"We must celebrate our good fortune, Herbie. And we shall!" Boris lifted a test tube. "In honor of the occasion, I have invented a new Magician's Fire. Orange version!"

A happy picture. Behind the two men, the mantelpiece stood, lined with newly taken photographs of the theater's performers—the Cossack dancers, the man who told jokes, Bruno the Strongman, and all the others, all in new outfits and with cheery expressions. But cheeriest of all were Herbie and Boris, reunited at last.

Harry felt a smile curve on his own face as he took in the happy pair and, in particular, the spindly shape of Herbie. *Herbie, who had started everything.* Down by his side, Harry's fingers were fluttering as he remembered that very first meeting in the middle of the New York winter, that trick with the flaming matches…

"Talking of magical powders and so on, Herbie…" Billie was trying to sound casual. "I don't suppose you'd finally consider giving us a few clues about some of those other tricks you do? The Bicycling over Spikes, perhaps? Spider up Sleeve?"

"It would be useful." Arthur chuckled. "Harry never did work anything out that night. Obviously, I know he's meant to figure them out himself, part of the game and all that. But a few hints would be most useful…"

"Would they, indeed?" Herbie Lemster chuckled as he helped Boris mix the contents of the test tube. "I'll think about it. But it strikes me that young Harry's perfectly skilled at unmasking secrets already. He exposed the truth of Wesley Jones's doings, didn't he? Not to mention making a few other discoveries along the way, I hear." He looked up. "Not about magic perhaps, but important nonetheless…"

Those wrinkle-surrounded eyes gleamed at Harry. They flicked over to Arthur and Billie, and then back to Harry again. The old magician's expression was mysterious, but to Harry the remark he had made was perfectly clear. Not much else was, because just then Boris chuckled and tilted the test tube, and with a thundering explosion, the room filled with orange smoke, thick and swirling. Billie waved at the plumes, Arthur wheezed, and Harry stumbled to the window, but by the time he had rattled it up and cleared the air, the two magicians had gone. *So much for clues about tricks.* He dropped back into his chair and counted the money inside the brown envelope Herbie had given him.

How things have changed. Harry lifted a hand and examined it through the smoke. Traces of boot polish stain could be seen on his fingertips, but that was all. Strange to think of the job he had once had, lugging that shoeshine box around in an attempt to earn a few cents. The shoeshine box was long-ago abandoned, and he had changed his lodgings, leaving behind the rather dilapidated boarding house of Mrs. Mack. *And it's not just me who's finding things a bit different.*

"How'd you think Mawkin's Glue Factory is managing without you, Billie?"

"Don't ask me. Never gone near the place, and I'm not planning to either." Billie flicked through the contents of her brown envelope too. "I'm done with gloop stirring. Same goes for all the other crummy work I've done—floor sweeping, garbage picking, and all the rest..."

"You really have done some terrible jobs, Billie." Arthur nodded thoughtfully.

"It's true. Come to think of it, nothing much about the road from New Orleans has been that easy, what with escaping from orphanages, trying to jump trains, and generally having to scratch a living together any way I could. Still, like I always say, it's not the sticky situations that matter; it's how you get out of them."

Another tap of the brown envelope, and there was a particularly wide grin on Billie's face, even by her standards. "And I don't think I've ever managed to wriggle my way out as spectacularly as this. Ending up in a real, proper job, doing stuff I actually like, and making some proper cash too!"

"You're right. We've found a pretty good earner,"

Arthur chipped in. "Not that I personally need the money, which is why I give most of it to the two of you." He pulled two handfuls of notes out of his envelope and handed one to Harry, the other to Billie. "Although I am going to keep a bit back, if that's all right, to help fund my new special membership cards to the Boston, Paris, and London libraries, in case I need books that aren't in New York. They'll mail them right to me, you know. Might be handy if we get around to thinking up some new tricks for the show."

"Absolutely, Artie…" Harry hesitated, remembering something. "By the way, the boarding school plan. Went off well?"

"Certainly did!" Arthur fished in his pockets. More paper ribbon spilled out, along with various envelopes and a book, which he thumped onto the table. *Techniques of Famous Forgers*, the title said. "So, that letter we snatched way back was just the beginning. Ever since, Father's servants have been writing letters to the school, and the school's been busily writing back, but none of those letters have ever arrived, because I've intercepted them, obviously.

"Picked up the school's ones as they fell through the mailbox, grabbed the servants' ones just before they were posted." He reached into another pocket and pulled out a little twisted length of metal. "This pick you made me for the mailbox outside my house came in handy, Harry."

"No problem." Harry smiled.

"So anyway, instead of the servants and the school getting the letters they expect, they're getting ones specially forged by me." As Arthur tapped the book, Harry saw no sign of the shadowy kink on his friend's forehead. "Just yesterday, the servants opened the very last letter from the school, in fact by me. It described all the final arrangements."

"Which were?"

"A cab called at the house just this morning. I boarded it with all my luggage, looking mournful and all that. But instead of taking me 452 miles away, like Father wanted, it brought me right here." Arthur jerked a thumb at a couple trunks piled in the corner of Herbie's office. "I thought I might make myself at home in one of the dressing rooms. Until the end of term, that is."

"What about the school?" asked Billie. "Won't they think it's odd when you don't arrive?"

"Not really because the last letter they got announced that Father had changed his mind and was sending me to a slightly cheaper school down the road from them instead. They'll be so annoyed that they'll just throw the letter in the trash. As for Father himself, I doubt he'll find out anytime soon. He's just set off on yet another business trip. Back to London, this time."

"London?"

"He'll be gone nearly six months. So it looks like he'll continue to pay no attention to me, boarding school or not." A frown, but it was a very slight one. "I know, it's a strange business. But the truth is, I've pretty much gotten used to it these days. Is it really such a bad thing, him wanting me out of his way? When it ends up with him accidentally having me sent to a place like this, where I can spend as much time as I like doing the best job in the world?" The frown was gone, and in its place was a grin as big as Billie's. "Not to mention doing it with the best friends in the world, eh?"

"Absolutely, Artie," said Harry.

He watched his friends. Billie was nodding at what Arthur had said, and had reached across and taken hold of his hand. Harry reached out and took hold of the other one. Arthur smiled, and Harry realized that, if he leaned forward, he could just reach across and grab Billie's spare hand. He did so, and for a moment the three of them sat like that, the fire beneath the mantelpiece warming them with its flickering glow. *Yes, things have turned out nicely*, Harry reflected…

And we've just gotten started.

Releasing his friends' hands and leaning back, he thought about what Arthur had said just now about researching new tricks. *Good point.* Thrilling though the Wesley Jones cage trick was, audiences would grow bored of it eventually, and new tricks would have to be devised, ones that were even more spectacular, even more death defying.

But that won't be so hard, Harry thought, feeling the warmth of the fire and glancing across at his friends, *Not as if I'm on my own.* Settling back in his chair, he started wondering what the next tricks would be…

"Master Harry? This just handed in for you at the stage door."

It was Bruno the Strongman. He was standing in the doorway, holding up an envelope. Harry rose from his chair and trod across the rug, his boots still warm. He took the letter and opened it as Bruno shuffled away. A sheet of paper, pale green in color, was inside. Burned into the bottom left corner, a symbol of a bird surrounded by black. And the letter's words were just as curious.

To Harry, Billie, and Arthur,

You have impressed us greatly. But your greatest achievements lie ahead of you—we will make sure of it.

Sent with the consent of
The Order of the White Crow

"The Order of the White Crow?" Arthur peered over Harry's shoulder.

"*We will make sure of it…*" Billie inspected the letter too. "What's that supposed to mean?"

Harry said nothing. He just let Billie slide the pale green paper out of his hands and headed for the window. *Just handed in at the stage door.* The sash was still open, and he leaned out of it, immediately remembering the tightrope walk into the Hotel Crosby and being thrown into air by the ecstatic crowd just a few days ago.

There he was. The man in the pale suit. The one Harry had glimpsed ten stories up, the one who had written in the notebook as the crowd cheered. He was standing just a short distance down the street, staring directly up at Herbie Lemster's office window. And he stayed like that, staring, as Harry felt a strange twitching sensation in the fingers of his right hand.

He held them up. Their tips were smeared with a pale green dust. Looking closer, he saw that the greenness seemed to have become part of the skin and that traces of it could even be seen underneath the skin, dissolving into the pinkness of his fingers. But he couldn't look at his hand any longer because his legs were feeling weak and he needed his hand to grip the wall. He heard two thuds behind him.

Unsteadily, he swung around. He saw Billie sprawled on the rug and Arthur collapsed in a chair. Both of them were unconscious, their heads lolling, their bodies limp. The pale green letter stood upright, pinched between Arthur's finger and thumb. Harry took a step forward, but his legs were even weaker, and his knees slammed into the rug. He crawled to his friends. They were still breathing. They almost looked quite peaceful as they lay there, sound asleep.

The door opened. Harry watched it and tried to look up, but his head was too heavy. He saw a pair of polished shoes and the hems of some pale suit trousers step into the room. They crossed to a point just a short distance from him.

"Your greatest achievements do indeed lie ahead

of you," a voice said. "You'll discover more shortly, when you wake up."

Harry tipped forward onto the rug. He landed right next to the polished shoes. He saw his own face reflected back to him in the gleaming leather. It was curved, out of shape. Who was this man? What was his purpose? Most importantly, what did he mean by "greatest achievements"? Harry felt those strange little twitches quivering through his body again, and his heart pounded as he readied himself for whatever lay ahead...

But, for the time being, his eyes flickered shut.

And he stopped seeing anything at all.

To be continued...

About the Author

Simon Nicholson grew up in Raynes Park, London. He worked in theater for a while before starting to write stories, mainly for children. Since then, he has written plays, books, and over a hundred episodes of children's television series, and has been nominated for BAFTA and RTS awards. He lives in Winchester with his young family—and lots of books about Houdini.